Jamaican Steppers

By

T. Anthony Johnson and K. M. Johnson

EAST ROAD PUBLISHING

National Harbor

ISBN-10: 0692333738
ISBN-13: 978-0692333730

EAST ROAD PUBLISHING, LLC
145 Fleet Street, Suite 167
National Harbor, MD 20745
www.EastRoadPublishing.com
ERPublishing@yahoo.com

DEDICATION

For Nettie Johnson, the Johnson and Bravo families, extended family and close friends from East Road, Kingston, Jamaica as well as other parts of Jamaica, the USA, and abroad for all the support that you have given which has made this novel possible.

Chapter 1

In the summer of 1987, on a hazy, hot morning in the Flatbush section of Brooklyn, New York, Chuckie decided to sleep late as he usually did on Mondays. The air conditioner, set on high, kept the apartment cool and comfortable, and lying next to him was his girlfriend, Dawn.

A loud knock startled Chuckie out of his half sleep. He eased the forty-four magnum from underneath his pillow and made his way to the door, dressed only in his silk boxers.

"Who dat?" he yelled.

"Stepper."

Chuckie unlocked the door to let his best friend into the apartment.

Stepper came into the entry hallway, which he had done on countless occasions.To his immediate left was the bathroom; a bit further down the hallway to the left was the kitchen; facing the front door of the apartment was the dining room; to the left of the dining room was the guest bedroom; and next to it was the main bedroom, which looked out into the living room. The apartment was immaculate. The living room floor was covered in a plush wall-to-wall white carpet, and a three piece luxury sofa set furnished the room. An assortment of fine paintings of different African animals and scenery hung on the mint green walls. The windows were covered with heavy off-white drapes, which, when closed, allowed a minimal amount of sunlight to enter the room. To the right of the drapes stood a large halogen lamp, and in the center of the room stood a heavy chrome and glass centerpiece. The rest of the apartment was decked out in similar tranquil fashion. Dawn took special pride in decorating the apartment when she and Chuckie moved in two years earlier, and she spared no expense.

Stepper always felt at home and secure when visiting his friends. He stretched out his right fist to meet Chuckie's with a light tap.

"Yo! A eleven o'clock in a de morning and you still in a bed? Dawn must a really a rub de pum-pum pon you!" They both laughed.

"Mek me tell you something my youth, you need fi find a good woman like Dawn, then you wouldn't up an' around this time a morning a talk foolishness."

"Mi brother, God no mek the woman yet weh can satisfy me. You fi understand seh mi is a bull an' full of too much energy fi one woman fi handle," said Stepper with a grin.

"Right now the only bull you a talk 'bout a bullshit," countered Chuckie. "Seriously speaking though, there's enough good women out there, but you always wind up wid de wrong one dem. I wan' see you find a good woman and start to have some little Steppers."

"Right now mi no ready for that life, and that life no ready for mi."

Chuckie was twenty-six years old, stood six feet five inches, and weighed a solid 240 pounds. Stepper was also twenty-six, though smaller in size. He stood five feet nine inches and weighed in at a lean 160 pounds. The two were best friends and had always had each other's back.

Each man was deadly in his own right; together they were a terror to many in the five Boroughs of New York, as well as a few states up and down the East Coast. Everywhere they went they left dead bodies or terrified victims in their wake.

Stepper arrived in the United States in 1970 at the age of ten and lived with his mother and father, along with three sisters and a younger brother. He lived and went to school in Newark, New Jersey and then later in East Orange, New Jersey. He dropped out of High School after his mother and father separated, and tried his hand at different jobs to help his mother make ends meet, but there was never enough money to pay the bills. He soon turned to part-time crime and later graduated to full-time criminal activity.

His mother and father maintained their culture in the household, so Stepper retained most of his heritage despite leaving Jamaica at such an early age. Most of Stepper's childhood friends were Jamaican also, and arrived in the United States from every parish in Jamaica. Most of these new immigrants made little to no attempt to assimilate into the American culture, which attracted Stepper even more, though he found himself more drawn to the tough guys coming out of Kingston.

Stepper attended only Jamaican parties, but while he was learning the American streets, he maintained a good relationship with a small select group of black

Americans. He learned quickly that there was big money in drugs, however, he despised hard drugs and had no respect for those who used them. Stepper sold only marijuana, which led to many run-ins with the law; both the Newark and East Orange Police Departments were well acquainted with him.

Chuckie arrived in the United States in 1976 at the age of sixteen. He was the only child of his mother with whom he lived in Orange, New Jersey. He attended Orange High School and graduated a year later.

Chuckie was bent on keeping the wrong company, and found it virtually impossible not to steal something. He maintained strong ties with many of his underworld friends from Jamaica, many of whom were arriving in New York each month. Chuckie was well known in Montego Bay, where he originated. As a youth, he had always kept company with the older rude boys of that community, and so he grew up rather quickly. He became known for having sticky fingers, which he took great pride in.

His mother made many sacrifices to bring him to America, fearing that if she didn't, his activities would result in his certain death. She tried her best to teach him to live a respectable life, but to no avail.

Stepper and Chuckie first encountered one another by chance one afternoon. While walking down Main Street in East Orange after cutting class, Chuckie had gone into Kings Supermarket intent on stealing something just because he felt like it. He walked up and down the aisles looking around, undecided as to what to steal, when he spotted Stepper. He knew right away that Stepper was Jamaican by the boastful way he walked. Chuckie approached and greeted him, then introduced himself. Each man felt the other's vibe and they took a strong liking to one another. Chuckie didn't steal anything that day; Stepper made his purchase and the two spent the rest of the day smoking marijuana. From that day on they formed an unbreakable bond.

They were both young, seventeen at the time, and crime was all they aspired to accomplish in their lifetimes. They were outlaws in the making and nothing but death could stop them from reaching their goal.

Stepper was the thinker of the two, and Chuckie was the muscle. Stepper, being small in stature, was known for pulling a trigger at the drop of a hat. Together they sold and smoked marijuana just about every day. They were inseparable, and all the Jamaicans in the neighborhood respected them and sought out their friendship.

Chuckie introduced Stepper to his friends, most of whom were well-known Jamaican underworld crime figures now living in New York and New Jersey. Stepper liked most of them, earned the respect of many of them, and soon he and Chuckie were hired by them to move large quantities of marijuana from New York to New Jersey. There they would sell it, pay off the Dons and make a profit for themselves. For a while everything ran like clockwork.

In 1984, however, things got hectic for Stepper and Chuckie. Two of the Jamaican Dons were murdered in New York, and soon after many of the soldiers started to fall victim to the crack cocaine epidemic. Those soldiers could no longer be relied on or trusted, so Chuckie and Stepper broke ties with them.

By that time the two of them had made enough

money to purchase their own marijuana. They made a good connection with a major dealer, got an extremely reasonable price on some high grade product, and started selling it by the pound. But soon jealousy set in among many of their longtime friends in New York.

In the summer of that year a few of those soldiers tried unsuccessfully to set up the two friends. In the weeks that followed, Chuckie and Stepper shot and wounded three of them. In retaliation, a few men from New York robbed Chuckie and Stepper's marijuana stash in New Jersey and were bent on killing them as well. Although Chuckie and Stepper were not at the apartment at the time, the robbers left a clear message by beating one of their workers unconscious. Chuckie and Stepper took it to heart and the war was on.

From that time on they spent most of their time at the marijuana spot maintaining security during the day while waging war against their enemies at night. Shootings became routine in and around their place of business. Soon the police were making daily raids in the neighborhood to crack down on the violence and drug activity.

Chuckie and Stepper were eventually arrested and charged with selling marijuana and illegal possession of firearms. The police could not link either of them to any of the shootings in the neighborhood, but had a strong case against them for selling drugs. Both men made bail quickly, and after serious consideration of their options decided to skip out on their bail and relocate to Brooklyn, New York.

The atmosphere in New York was ripe for them to grow their drug business. Crack had taken a major hold on the city, and money was everywhere. It wasn't long before Stepper changed his long held view about hard drugs. For him it became all about money.

They were still at war with some of their old crew, however, and found themselves in numerous shootouts on far too many occasions. Consequently, their prospects for selling drugs in New York didn't last for long, and they soon turned all their attention to full-time robbery and gunning for their enemies. In less than a year, most of their enemies were dead at their hands, though they soon realized it was impossible to hang up their guns for good, as every new shooting and robbery produced new enemies.

"Yo, I man pulled down pon a police boy last night and tek him gun off a him, de joker eye dem almost pop out a him head when him see de nine a point in a him face," said Stepper, excited.

"What! Mek me see it," said Chuckie.

Stepper handed him a blue steel thirty-eight police revolver.

"Yo! It nice, we have fi get some extra teeth fi this."

"You right, I wan' run this red hot before we get rid a it."

"How you get de drop pon him?" asked Chuckie.

"You wan' see, last night me go check de gyal Carol round a Kings Highway."

"Yo, me a tell you fi stop go round deh, you done know seh we an' de boy Sammy in a war fi years."

"Dem boy deh can't stop me from go look fi I gyal." He continued, "As me did a seh, as me lef her house and walk up de street fi go a I car, nuh this white police boy me see a come towards me like him wan' gi' me a check. De boy a look me down hard, me check seh a because me

7

have on me vest and look kind a bulky. Me brother, me just walk up pon de pussy and back me nine pon him. De boy eye pop out a him head, me tell de boy, pussy you arm and me arm, you have on you vest and me have on me vest, draw! De pussy hold up him two hand dem and a beg, 'bout him a officer of de law an' me no fi do nothing me a go regret. Me put de nine in a him face and ease out him gun and tell de pussy fi run, then me empty a clip in a de air. Mek me tell you, me never see a boy run so fast in a me life, Don Quarrie was a boy to him last night."

The men burst out laughing.

At the 71st Precinct, Officer Anthony McCoy sat mulling over books upon books of police photos in an attempt to find a mug shot of the man, or men, as his story went, who held him up and stole his service revolver. After sitting since 2:00 a.m. that morning, he stiffly raised up from his chair to stretch when he noticed Lt. John Fisher heading in his direction.

"Any luck?"

"No Lieutenant."

"The Captain wants you in his office."

Officer McCoy followed the Lieutenant into the Captain's office.

"McCoy! Did you come across any of them in the books?"

"No Captain."

"Sit down." The Captain motioned toward a chair. "I want to hear the entire story from the beginning."

McCoy had already told the story to different teams of officers a dozen times since the incident occurred, but this would be his first time telling it to the Captain. He stuck to the story he had made up; if he revealed the truth, the rest of the men in the department would ridicule him and make his life a living hell.

"I was on patrol when I noticed some suspicious activity in the vicinity of the 1800 block of Kings Highway. There were two individuals acting suspiciously and it looked like a drug exchange was being made. I exited my vehicle and approached the two suspects. As I did, three or four other men came out of nowhere with weapons drawn. The two men whom I approached also produced weapons. The bastards were all Jamaicans and they were wearing bulletproof vests, Captain; they were ready for a fire fight. One of them stuck an M-16 assault rifle in my face. I couldn't do anything. They had me cornered, and one of them took my service revolver. Then they backed away from me and fired about thirty shots from what I think was the assault rifle. I had to duck and dive for cover in order to save my life. I don't know why I wasn't hit."

"Those sons-of-bitches," said Capt. McKenny, "they were wearing vests! We'll get those punks dead or alive. If it's a fire fight they want, we'll give it to them. I've already placed a call to our Five Boroughs boys in Manhattan to come in and assist us on this. I'm expecting them to arrive within the hour, and I've asked them to bring mug shots of all the Jamaican hoodlums they have on file. You need to call your wife and let her know you'll be home late tonight. I want you here when they arrive, and I want you to give them your full cooperation. I want that gun off the streets and back in our hands before the day is out, and those punks behind bars! And Lieutenant," he continued harshly, "I want you to personally pay a visit to those punks in the 90s and let them know that no marijuana will be sold in that neighborhood until we recover that gun and their punk friends who assaulted my officer. I don't want a joint coming out of that neighborhood! Is that clear?"

"Yes sir!"

"Chuckie! Who dat out deh wid you?" shouted Dawn from the bedroom.

"A Stepper," replied Chuckie.

Stepper made his way to the bedroom where Dawn was tucked in the bed under the covers. "Dawn, when you a go hook me up with you fat ass friend Pat?"

"She already have a man."

"Dat never stop me before."

"Me have a nice girl me wan' you fi meet."

"Alright, me want you fi hook that up fi me."

Chuckie walked into the bedroom and reclined next to Dawn. Stepper stood in the doorway.

"Chuckie, mek we tek a ride go check Cow over pon Ocean Ave, him have a works fi we," said Stepper.

"Right now, you know how I man feel 'bout go out pon de road pon a Monday, especially in a de morning."

"How you so superstitious?"

"Call me wah you want, but me a tell you, de police boy dem always a look fi make an arrest after coming off a de weekend," said Chuckie.

"Right now, we can' make dat stop we from eat food, from food fi get tek food fi get tek, no matter de time or de day a de week."

"Yo, you done know say me have a gun warrant pon me a Westchester County, and by now dem must know say de gun have a body pon it."

"Me brother, me have warrant pon me a Delaware,

and de two a we have one a New Jersey, you think say me a mek dem wicked boy deh stop me from do wah me have fi do fi survive, I nah tek no check from no police boy. Gear up and mek we tek a ride!"

Chuckie knew his friend was right and meant every word he said, there was no way the police would take him alive, and being his best friend, no matter what, he preferred to be there next to him if anything went down. Chuckie got up and went into the bathroom.

Dawn kept quiet throughout the conversation. She knew not to come between these two men. She was a trooper in the highest sense of the word, and she knew quite well how extremely tight these men were and that they would always take care of each other.

"Yo Chuckie!" Stepper called out, "Weh de Mac-ten deh?"

"You wan' see, me lef' it wid Dreaddy a Bushwick, and de next one deh a Bronx wid Pops," replied Chuckie.

Dreaddy and Pops were their two main sidekicks. Dreaddy was the eldest of the four men. He was 30 years old and built like a bull at five feet eight inches and 220 pounds. He kept his hair close cut, was of a dark complexion, and rarely smiled. He earned the name Dreaddy from the fear he instilled in most people. He and Pops were extremely loyal to Stepper and Chuckie. Pops was the youngest of the four. He was a well-built six foot one inch twenty year old, and he weighed 190 lbs. He wore his hair in braids most of the time and his complexion was high yellow.

"So wah Pops a gwaan wid, me no see or hear from him in a while?" asked Stepper.

"Him come check I one day last week, him breed off a thing and him and her a live together. Plus, de weed house weh him fly off a Gunn Hill Road a pick up and a keep him busy."

"Me feel good fi know dat, you know me check fi dah youth deh."

"If everything go smooth me want we fi flash go check him later," said Chuckie.

"Yea mon, me well wan' see him still. Me wan' we check Dreaddy later and pick up de Mac-ten after we check Cow."

"As you a talk 'bout that, Dreaddy say him have a works him wan' mash in a Bushwick."

"Wah kind a money him a talk 'bout?" asked Stepper.

"Him a show I say de boy Danny have a coke house weh a make a bag a money in a Bushwick."

"Well we haffi look in a dat, you done know how I feel 'bout dem boy deh, even though him never down wid him crackhead friend dem weh draw card pon we a New Jersey an' rob we spot, a still him friend dem. We owe him a pay back fi him friend dem. A long time me a tell you seh dem boy deh fi get hold."

Chuckie made his way back to the bedroom and chose a neatly pressed pair of pants and a tight fitting shirt from the closet. Then he retrieved his bulletproof vest from the dresser drawer and slowly eased into it, making sure all the straps were in place. He placed his forty-four magnum into the drawer and retrieved his nine millimeter along with three extra clips. He picked up a silver chain which he rubbed and kissed before putting it around his neck; it was his voodoo chain that he purchased from a Cuban Voodoo woman. He paid her a thousand dollars for her services and she made it clear to him that the chain would protect him and warn him whenever he was in danger; Chuckie believed every word of it. He stood in front of the mirror admiring his chain as Stepper watched him in dismay and shook his head.

"Boy you strange no rawtid fi believe in a dem foolishness deh. All de protection you need a de vest you have on an' you gun."

Chuckie kissed his teeth then went over to Dawn, kissed her, and assured her that he would see her later.

The men left the apartment, each carrying a nine millimeter and three extra magazines. Stepper also carried the thirty-eight police revolver. Little did either of them know that this would be one of the longest and bloodiest Mondays of their entire lives.

Chapter 2

Chuckie and Stepper decided to take Chuckie's brown 1986 Volvo Sedan and leave Stepper's 1985 BMW Sedan where it was parked on Snyder Avenue. Chuckie led the way to his car with Stepper bringing up the rear a few paces behind. The two were never in the habit of walking side by side, especially in Brooklyn. They had far too many enemies who were just as deadly as they were.

Chuckie got in his car and unlocked the passenger door as Stepper approached and got in. Chuckie put the car in drive and made his way up New York Avenue to Church Avenue.

"Yo Chuckie, mek we flash go a Bushwick go check Dreaddy before we go check Cow, I wan' have de Mac-ten wid me when we check Cow. Plus, it would a better we have it pon de works."

"Yea, mek we do dat, me know Dreaddy well wan' see we anyway."

The men made a right turn onto Rogers Avenue from Church, then made their way down Rogers heading towards Atlantic Avenue.

"It a go be one hot Rawtid day today, it already ninety degrees, and de damn vest make it feel like a hundred and twenty," said Chuckie.

They both wore bulletproof vests, as had been their practice for the past few months. They had witnessed far too many shootings in and around Brooklyn to be caught without their vests, especially during the summer months.

"Yea, it hot, especially wid de vest on, but dem vest yah wi' keep man alive. A mid August we in a and people blood a boil, an' you know when black people blood a boil gunshot fly. Right now soldiers haffi pad up fi stay alive."

Chuckie reached over and flipped the air conditioner up to high.

As they continued down Rogers Avenue, Stepper spotted a guy standing in front of Club Jamaica Inn, which was also a bar.

"Chuckie, no de boy Roy dat a lean up pon dah blue Benz deh?"

"Rawtid! A de bloodclot boy yes. Him a sleep." Chuckie rolled down his window and disengaged the safety on his nine millimeter.

Stepper reached over, stopped him, and gave him the thirty-eight police revolver. "Yo, me bredda, anything a get pitch today, a get pitch in a police style."

Chuckie reengaged the safety on his nine millimeter, placed it underneath his right thigh, and picked up the thirty-eight revolver Stepper had placed on his lap.

As they approached Roy, Chuckie held the thirty-eight in his right hand with his left hand still on the steering wheel. He cocked the gun as he came to a full stop parallel to Roy. Roy's back was turned to the traffic and he seemed like he didn't have a care in the world; big mistake. Chuckie squeezed off two quick bursts from the thirty-eight, and Roy fell flat on his face, dead before he hit the pavement. A gaping hole was all that remained between his nose and forehead, along with another hole just below his Adam's apple. Chuckie stepped on the gas. "De pussy fi dead long time."

In less than ten minutes after leaving Chuckie's apartment, the police revolver had claimed its first victim. The men continued down Rogers, made a right turn onto Atlantic Avenue and continued their journey to Bushwick.

Six months prior to Roy's murder, it was Chuckie who had been caught sleeping. He had an affair with an attractive Jamaican girl by the name of Ann Marie. During one of their many conversations he discovered that she was on a friendly basis with Roy's boss, Mackie, who was believed to be worth two to three million dollars from his cocaine and marijuana businesses in Brooklyn and Queens. An idea immediately sparked in Chuckie's head as he quickly saw his golden opportunity. He and Stepper had been trying to get their hands on this guy for quite some time, but could never find him or where he lived. They tailed him one night leaving a club, but lost him on the Belt Parkway; they vowed to get him one day.

Ann Marie was a party girl by nature who frequented different clubs in and around Brooklyn and Queens, which is how they met. He was attracted to her at first sight with her light complexion – a result of her Indian heritage, long black hair and killer smile. She walked as if she was walking on clouds, and had a body that men would die for. Chuckie soon discovered she was a teaser and a schemer, a bad girl who was attracted to bad men, who dreamed of getting rich and living large. He fell in love with all her qualities, good and bad, and had been seeing her for the past year. Stepper, on the other hand, didn't think too highly of her and felt she couldn't be trusted.

Chuckie knew he could easily convince Ann Marie to go along with his plan, but he had to be careful, not knowing how close she was to Mackie. Mackie and his crew were known to be hard core killers, but that didn't faze Chuckie and his crew; all their enemies were known killers.

"So wha' a gwaan wid you and Mackie?" Chuckie asked Ann Marie.

"Wah you mean wha' a gwaan between me and him?"

"So wah, me can't ask you no question, after all, you a my gyal. I no wan' get nasty wid him fi a look you."

Ann Marie laughed, taking great delight in seeing her man get jealous. "No, No, a nuh nothing like dat. Me and him baby mother, Pam, used to go a school together a yard, a so me get fi know him."

"So you know him from yard?"

"Me never too like him back then, me just use to see him when him come 'round; him use to always a beat Pam."

"So wah you and him have now?" asked Chuckie.

"Me hook him up wid some travel documents from time to time and him pay me good money fi dem."

By this time Chuckie knew exactly how he was going to put his plan into action. "Ann Marie, me have some documents me a try sell fi a long time, you check say Mackie would a interested in a dem?"

"Me know seh a talk you a talk, wah you really wan' wid him?"

"Alright, me nah play no games wid you, a long time me wan' hold de boy."

"Me no in a dat, me no wan' nobody come kill me off," said Ann Marie.

"Nobody nah come kill you off, you think me would a mek nobody come do you anything. Listen, a long time you a talk 'bout you wan' go live a Florida, this a you chance fi get a bag a money and flash lef' New York once and for all."

Ann Marie was paying close attention by this time. She had always entertained the thought of getting someone to rob Mackie. She often considered asking Chuckie but she just couldn't build up enough courage to ask him. She knew Mackie was worth a lot of money, so this was the opportunity she had been dreaming of for so long. "So how much money me wi' get if me decide fi do it?"

Chuckie thought long and hard before answering. He had to give her a figure she couldn't refuse, and he also didn't want to lie to her. "Listen baby, if me get de kind a money weh me know me can get from de boy, me wi' gi' you fifty thousand dollars, plus enough weed and coke fi you start you own business a Florida."

Ann Marie's eyes sparkled and Chuckie knew he had her.

"Alright, just tell me wah you wan' me fi do."

Chuckie smiled. This job would be easy pickings. He told Ann Marie his plan. First he had to get in touch with a few of his soldiers, then she would call Mackie and tell him she had some documents for him. Mackie was in the habit of buying old green cards, which he used to bring up members of his old gang from Jamaica. He would pick them up at her house, at which time Chuckie and his crew would be in the apartment waiting to kidnap him and take him to his 'stash house.' It was believed that

Mackie was sitting on hundreds of thousands of dollars in that stash house, but very few people knew where it was located.

The trap was easily set and Mackie took the bait. Since he had done business with Ann Marie on numerous occasions before, with everything going smoothly, his mind was at ease and nothing seemed out of the ordinary to him when Ann Marie called to tell him she had a set of documents for sale. He didn't think twice about it and agreed to pick them up from her later that evening.

It took Chuckie two days to put it all together before allowing Ann Marie to place the call to Mackie. Chuckie brought in Stepper, Dreaddy and Pops. Now all they had to do was wait for Mackie to get there. Mackie arrived at Ann Marie's apartment at 8:00 p.m. that Friday. Ann Marie answered the knock on the door. "Who Dat?"

"Who you a expect, a me Mackie." Mackie was accompanied by one of his bodyguards.

Ann Marie unlocked the door and led them to the living room. Before the men could react, Chuckie, Stepper, Dreaddy and Pops were on them with guns drawn. Chuckie slapped Mackie across his face with the butt of his gun sending Mackie sprawling to the ground.

Stepper placed his gun directly to the bodyguard's head. "Don't even breathe boy." Dreaddy then moved in, frisked both men and relieved them of a pair of nine millimeters.

Stepper and Pops tied up both men using electric cords on their legs and wrists. Chuckie focused his full attention on Mackie. "Hay, boy! A long time me wan' hold you eno! Me ago ask you one time and one time only, how much you life worth to you?"

"Me only have a small money left right now, me just

use all a me cash bail a youth out a jail," replied Mackie.

Whap! Chuckie slapped him across the face with his gun.

Mackie spat out blood, his lips bleeding badly from the blow.

"Me no wan' hear none a dat fuckery from you! All I wan' you fi tell me is weh de stash house deh and how much money you have in deh."

This went on for almost an hour with Mackie taking a severe beating before he finally broke. "Alright! Alright! If me gi' you de money, you wi' mek we live?"

"Listen to me boy, wah me ago kill unnu fa, when as long as unnu alive me can come tax unnu again. You have me word, as long as me get de money me nah kill unnu."

"Alright, me wi' tek unnu go a de spot," said Mackie.

"How much money deh deh?" asked Stepper.

"About $200,000."

"Gi' me de address," demanded Dreaddy.

"756-23 Carol Street, second floor."

"Is a private house?" asked Stepper.

"Yea, is a two family house."

"Who live pon de first floor?" asked Chuckie.

"De landlady wid her family."

"Alright, a little after nine o'clock right now, I don't wan' go over deh till about one or two in a de morning, by then de landlady a sleep," said Chuckie. The men had no intention of letting Mackie and his bodyguard live; they knew very well that Mackie was a killer and that they had to play for keeps with him. Besides, Chuckie and Stepper didn't work that way; they had stayed alive all these years because of their willingness to kill those who would kill them, and they knew that Mackie would not hesitate for a second to wipe them out.

To kill some time the men decided to take the bodyguard over to Mackie's house. Mackie, under the severe beating, had given up the location of his house rather than the location of his stash house. He told the men his wife was at home and there was about $60,000 in cash and a pair of forty-five Mac-tens along with some drugs. Stepper wanted those guns even more than he wanted the $60,000; in case things didn't go as planned at the stash house, at least they would have the guns and the $60,000. It would later prove to be the best decision they had made that night, and it would prove to be a blessing for Mackie and his bodyguard, Harry.

"Harry, mek me tell you right now, if you try anything, me ago put a bullet right in a you head, and come back yah so and brush you boss," said Chuckie.

Harry assured them he wouldn't try anything.

Chuckie, Stepper, and Dreaddy led Harry out of the apartment, leaving Pops and Ann Marie behind to keep an eye on Mackie. Chuckie brought the car up to the front of the building, and Stepper and Dreaddy led Harry over to the car. The men piled into the car. Stepper sat next to Harry with his gun trained on Harry's head.

"Harry, when we reach a de house, we ago walk up wid you a de door, I wan' you fi ring de bell and get Mackie gyal fi open de door, no bother pull no shit!" said Chuckie.

"Everything cool," replied Harry.

Everything went as planned. Harry rang the bell and Mackie's wife, Pam, answered the door. The men barged into the apartment holding Pam at gunpoint. She didn't resist but was clearly shaken up. Harry rested his hand on her shoulder and assured her that everything would be all right.

Chuckie ordered both of them to sit on the sofa in the living room, holding them at bay with his gun. "Gyal! Weh de money deh?

"Me no have no money in a de house!"

Chuckie slapped her across her face with the back of his hand. "Listen Gyal, me nah ask you again, you man send me fi de money, and if me no get it, you, him and unnu friend yah so dead!"

"Pam tell him weh it deh, Mackie already tell dem seh him have sixty thousand dollars in a de house," said Harry.

"Alright, Alright! Everything in a de bedroom closet under de box dem."

Stepper was already searching the bedroom when Chuckie called out to him to check the closet. He opened the closet door and, to his surprise, there were boxes and boxes of clothes and different items packed neatly and sealed, ready to be shipped to Jamaica. He quickly brushed them aside and came upon two large suitcases. He pulled them from the closet and opened them. Each of them contained fifty pounds of marijuana, but there was no money. He went back into the closet and removed more boxes, then he came upon a strongbox. He retrieved the strongbox and demanded the key from Pam. She gave it to him and when he opened the box it contained two kilograms of cocaine and many stacks of bills. There were mostly hundreds and fifties, totaling about $72,000. Stepper kept searching and found the pair of Mac-ten and three nine millimeters, along with boxes and boxes of ammunition.

Stepper did a more detailed search of the house which revealed barrels and boxes of brand new clothing, labeled and ready to be shipped to Jamaica. Stepper figured that Mackie must own a few stores in Jamaica.

Along with the money and drugs, the men also retrieved hundreds of thousands of dollars worth of jewelry. In all, it was one of the best jobs they had pulled off in a long time, but they knew that the mother of the haul was still awaiting them at the stash house.

The problem now was what to do with Harry and Pam. Killing them was out of the question, at least not until they were able to get their hands on the money in the stash house. They decided to take them both back to Ann Marie's apartment.

"Dreaddy, tek de weed out a de suitcase dem an' put it in a some garbage bags so it fit in a de car trunk, then lock off everything in a de car trunk before we bring dem out," said Chuckie.

Dreaddy went to the kitchen and returned with a few garbage bags which he doubled and filled with the drugs and money, then took them to the car and secured them.

Stepper, in the mean time, loaded one of the Mac-tens and kept it close.

Dreaddy returned to the apartment and signaled the men that everything was secured.

Chuckie walked Pam out first and secured her in the front seat of the Volvo, fastening her seat belt around her before taking the driver's seat next to her. Then Stepper and Dreaddy emerged from the building with Harry in tow. They positioned him between them in the middle of the back seat.

Chuckie drove cautiously as he made his way back to Ann Marie's apartment. He was careful not to draw attention or get pulled over by the police, which would have been the last thing they needed.

They arrived back at Ann Marie's apartment at about 11:00 p.m. and everything was in order. The men secured Harry and Pam by tying them up, hands and legs, then Pops and Dreaddy retrieved the drugs and money from the car. They spent the next two hours counting the money and smoking spliffs. Ann Marie was in Paradise; she had never seen so much money before in her life.

"Mackie," said Stepper, "wah you a do wid all a dem clothes deh an' food you have in a you house?"

"Me a send dem go a Yard."

"Wah you ago do, sell them?"

"No, me have nuff people out deh fi tek care of, nuff a dem a depend pon me. Everything you see in a I house a fi de poor people dem," replied Mackie.

Stepper was impressed; he had just returned from vacationing in Jamaica six months earlier, and he was saddened by the level of poverty he saw in the ghettos there. So much, in fact, that he gave away everything he had in his possession and returned with only the clothes on his back. When Chuckie picked him up at the airport, Stepper told him how the people were suffering, and that everyone he met wanted to come to America to escape the poverty. Shortly after that, both men put together a few barrels full of clothing and supplies and shipped them to their families and friends. It made them feel good and they vowed to continue helping in that way.

By 2:00 a.m. the men decided to make their move. The plan was to take Mackie to the stash house and leave Harry and Pam behind.

"Dreaddy, me wan' you hold down de fort, and mek Pops ride wid me and Stepper," said Chuckie. Chuckie felt it best to leave the older and more experienced man to watch over the two hostages rather than to give the younger Pops the added responsibility. Pops was fully capable, but at this junction in the game Chuckie didn't want to take any chances. Dreaddy already knew the rationale in Chuckie's thinking without elaborating on it. They had pulled off many jobs together and had a clear understanding of one another's thought process.

Stepper understood without saying a word and so did Pops. Pops had learned a lot in the past from these two men, so he continued to trust their decisions. Before leaving the apartment, Chuckie warned Mackie to be on his best behavior.

"Mackie," said Chuckie, "Harry and you woman keep dem cool and never do nothing fi put you life in a danger, knowing seh we have you, so, no bother do nothing fi put dem lives in a danger! You understand wah me a seh?"

"All me wan' know say unnu nah go kill we after you get all a de money."

"As I man tell you before, I nah go do unnu nothing as long as I get de money."

Mackie didn't believe him for a minute, he knew these men would kill them, they couldn't afford not to, but he had to buy some time and try to find a way out. The money wasn't an issue at this point, the only thing that mattered to him right now was staying alive. "Alright, me wi' do wah you wan'."

The men then left the apartment with Mackie in tow. Chuckie got the car and brought it parallel to the front of the building. As he pulled up, Stepper was in front with Mackie in the middle and Pops held onto Mackie's arm, as the three of them made their way to the car. Suddenly Mackie shook free from Pops' grip and made a mad dash up the street. Pops was right behind him with gun in hand. Stepper jumped in the passenger seat as Chuckie made a u-turn and bore down on Mackie. Mackie ran into a back yard with Pops right on his heels. Pops dived on top of Mackie and they both hit the ground hard. As Mackie tried to wrestle Pops' gun away from him, Stepper came running up and pistol whipped Mackie over his head, nearly knocking him unconscious. They dragged him back to the waiting car and returned to Ann Marie's apartment where they tied him up and beat him senseless.

"You is one wicked bloodclot boy, you willing fi mek you woman and you friend dead fi save you skin!" said Stepper.

Dreaddy was pissed and continued to whip on Mackie until Chuckie pulled him off. "Yo, we no have no time fi this, I no wan' blow de works," said Chuckie.

"So wah we ago do now?" asked Dreaddy.

"Mek we tek Harry over de spot and lef de boy yah, we done have de key fi de house."

The men parked a few houses down the street from the stash house. Stepper checked his watch, it was 3:00 a.m. They made their way up the flight of stairs to the front door of the house. Chuckie inserted the key and opened the front door. To his surprise the landlady greeted them at her apartment door, which was located to the immediate right of the front door. She and a few members of her family were up watching movies and drinking.

She recognized Harry but seemed somewhat taken aback by the presence of the three strangers who accompanied him. "Harry," she asked, "where is Mackie?"

"Oh, I was expecting to meet him here," replied Harry.

Then he made a sudden move that caught everyone by surprise. He began inching his way up to the woman's front door in an attempt to enter her apartment. She was shocked by his sudden move, but before she could react, Chuckie put his arm around Harry's shoulder and said, "Since Mackie no deh yah mek we come back later in the day."

Harry knew that if he resisted, as every fiber of his body was telling him to do, he and the landlady would be dead. Not that he cared one way or the other about her life, his only concern was saving his own. He quickly realized that there was no way out for him; his best bet was to remain cool for the time being. He said good-bye to the landlady and he and the men left the building.

Chuckie, Stepper and Pops were furious; the works had been blown. Chuckie wanted to kill Harry, but Stepper convinced him not to, that there was still a chance of pulling it off the next day.

Back at the apartment the men sat down and went over all their options. They came to the conclusion that the plan was dead in its tracks. It was too risky to keep the three hostages on ice for the better part of the day. Someone may miss them and start putting two and two together. Chuckie called Stepper over to a corner in the room to talk out of earshot of the three hostages.

"Stepper, mek we brush dem an' wrap this thing up."

"Yo! We can' kill dem," replied Stepper.

"Wah you a talk 'bout?"

"Listen, if we kill dah youth deh, God an' nature a go turn 'gainst we. Dah youth deh a do nuff good things fi people a Yard and as me tell you, de people dem a suffer out deh."

"Me brother, if we let dem go, we and dem ago in a war fi years fi come."

"Since when we start worry 'bout dat? Dem bredda deh haffi respect we, dem know say we know weh fi find dem, an' dem know killers when dem see killers, trust me pon dah one yah."

"Alright! But me ago talk to dem an' see wah kind a vibes me get from dem, just play along wid me," said Chuckie.

Chuckie went back over to the three hostages. "Mackie, this a it, me tell you if me get de money I wi' mek unnu live, but de way I see it, it look like unnu prefer de money over unnu lives."

"Me know unnu did a go kill we anyway, wid or wid-out de money," replied Mackie.

Chuckie picked up a pillow, cocked his gun and placed the pillow on top of Mackie's head. Mackie slowly turned to his wife and friend, told them that he loved them and said good-bye. He didn't beg or plead for his life, but showed great courage in meeting his fate; a rare thing that impressed Stepper and the others. Stepper's respect grew tenfold for Mackie and deep down he wished Mackie was a part of their crew.

They all looked at Mackie a little differently now – more as a soldier rather than a selfish joker just out to make a lot of money for himself.

Chuckie removed the gun and pillow from Mackie's head. "Listen, one thing save unnu life tonight, an' dat a wah you a do fi de people dem a Yard, you lucky we go a you house and see all a dem things deh weh you have fi send go deh, dat and only dat saved you life. If we haffi go a war wid you, you best know say nothing nah save you life next time, it in a you hands now an' right now it no matter to me one way or the other wah you choose because I love de war game," said Chuckie.

"I nah go start no beef over this, de man dem can keep everything," said Mackie. He felt a great deal of respect for these men because of the care they showed about the suffering back home in Jamaica, which was something he was passionate about. Far too many Jamaicans never looked back to reach out and help those they left behind.

The men cleared out the loot they had in the apartment before letting them go.

Mackie kept his word, there was no retaliation for the robbery. Ann Marie was given $10,000, a half kilo of cocaine, and twenty pounds of Marijuana as her cut for setting up Mackie. She continued to live at the same apartment with Chuckie's assurance that she didn't have to fear Mackie, and Chuckie continued to spend time with her at the apartment as often as possible to reassure her.

The four men split up the rest of the money, marijuana, and cocaine among themselves. Mackie let things die down and there was no war. However, a month after the robbery Chuckie pulled up in front of Club Jamaica Inn, where Mackie and his crew hung out and asked to see Mackie. He was told that Mackie was not there, so he entered the bar for a drink. After a few shots of white rum he began disrespecting a few of Mackie's boys in the club – a major slipup. Two of Mackie's boys, Roy and Mafia, both of whom were totally against Mackie's decision to let the robbery die, took serious offense to what Chuckie was doing. They sat in a dark corner of the bar and Chuckie was unaware of their presence. At the onset the two men were trying their best not to get into anything with Chuckie, but his disrespecting their friends was more than they were willing to take. Roy blew his top, pulled his gun and, with Mafia following him, crept up on Chuckie and opened fire. Chuckie was hit twice in his right leg as he returned fire. He was able to make it to his car and drove himself to Brooklyn Hospital. He was released the following day on crutches. The bullets went in and out, nothing serious, just flesh wounds, but Chuckie's pride was damaged. The incident led to the start of hostilities even though the shooting was not sanctioned by Mackie who accused Roy and Mafia of overreacting.

Stepper was ticked off but when he found out what led to the shooting, he went off on Chuckie. Chuckie knew his friend was right to be pissed off at him. He knew it was a foolish move on his part, one that could have cost him his life. Stepper cooled off after a while, and although he was pissed off at Roy and Mafia, he didn't harbor any ill feelings towards Mackie. He knew Mackie hadn't been at the bar and if he had been, the shooting would probably never have occurred.

Stepper decided not to go hunting for Mackie and his boys, and he made that clear to Chuckie, but they agreed that if they ever ran into Roy or Mafia they would gun them down. They wouldn't include Mackie in the vendetta, however, as long as he continued to hold up to his end of the bargain.

Neither Roy nor Mafia were seen by Stepper or Chuckie until that fateful Monday morning six months later, when they caught Roy sleeping at his post.

Chapter 3

Lieutenant John Fisher had been with the police force for the past twenty years. He came from a white upper middle class family, and the last thing they wanted was for him to join the police force. John decided to go against their wishes and pursued a career in law enforcement.

Sergeant Harry Fuller, on the other hand, came from a poor black family in Harlem. He witnessed crime all around him throughout his childhood and those experiences are what drove him to join the police force. He felt it was a way for him to contribute to the betterment of his people and family, on the whole. While with the police force for twelve years he had made countless arrests while climbing the ranks to become a sergeant. He and Lieutenant Fisher had teamed up for the past two years, developing a strong bond. Together they solved many difficult cases and, in doing so, had earned the respect of their commanders. They were known by their peers as the salt and pepper, Starsky and Hutch.

Lieutenant Fisher and Sergeant Fuller had just pulled

out of the police parking lot when a call came in over the radio of a shooting in front of Club Jamaica Inn on Rogers Avenue.

"Harry," said Lieutenant Fisher, "let's take that call."

Sergeant Fuller hit the siren, placed the emergency flashing light on top of his unmarked car, and stepped on the gas. Lieutenant Fisher picked up the radio and notified the base that they were en route to the crime scene. In less than two minutes they arrived at the scene. There were already two squad cars there, along with two detectives from the homicide squad.

Lieutenant Fisher walked over to speak to the detectives. "Majors, who's the corpse?"

"We haven't ascertained that as of yet Lieutenant," replied Detective Bruce Majors.

"It appears to be a drive-by. We have no witness to the shooting," said Detective Bernard O'Connor.

The Lieutenant walked over to the body and took a closer look at the victim. "Majors," he said, "it appears he's been hit twice. He's wearing one of those rasta, red, yellow, and green, belts. Everything about him says Jamaican. I want everything you got on this guy."

"I'll get all the information to you as soon as I get it Lieutenant."

People crowded around trying to get a look at the body, but the uniformed officers kept them at bay as they quickly secured the area with yellow crime scene tape. Soon the coroner arrived at the scene.

One of the officers taking pictures found what looked like a bullet hole right above the door of the bar. "Detective Majors, take a look at this."

Detective Majors and his partner headed over to the door where the uniformed officer stood pointing at a hole. "Looks like a bullet hole. Have our lab boys remove it and get it to ballistics."

Lieutenant Fisher joined the men to take a closer look at the bullet hole. "Majors, I want you to get in touch with me as soon as you get the ballistics on this shooting along with a full report."

"Will do, Lieutenant."

The Lieutenant headed to his vehicle followed by Sergeant Fuller. "Fuller, lets head into the 90s, we have to deliver the Captain's message to the Rastas."

Sergeant Fuller started up the engine and hit the gas pedal, pulling the vehicle away from the curb. He headed in the direction of Atlantic Avenue, made a right turn and continued to Utica Avenue.

"Fisher," said Sergeant Fuller, "what's your take on that shooting?"

"I don't know, but I want to pay very close attention to anything having to do with Jamaicans for the rest of this week. I damn sure don't like the idea of a bunch of them going around wearing bulletproof vests and disarming police officers. They've crossed the god damn line this time!"

Across town, two well-dressed detectives entered the 71st Precinct, showed their badges to the desk sergeant and said that Captain McKenny was expecting them. They were led to the Captain's office.

"Captain, I'm Detective James Buchanan, and this is Detective Derrick Bradley from the Special Crime Task Force. Our Captain briefed us on the current situation."

"Come on in and have a seat gentlemen," said Captian McKenny. "I've been expecting you. I have a serious problem here that has the potential to affect the morale of my men. Apparently there are a bunch of Jamaican punks wearing bulletproof vests and carrying high powered automatic rifles on the streets of my city. They've held up one of my officers, Officer McCoy, and stolen his service revolver. Officer McCoy has been going through our photo lineup all morning without any success. I'm committing the full weight of this department to bringing those thugs to justice and recovering my officer's revolver. I need everything you have on Jamaicans who may fit that profile. I want you guys to work closely with Officer McCoy. Have him take a look through your photos and see if he comes up with anything. I have a feeling those punks may not be from Brooklyn, at least not from the neighborhood where the crime occurred; my officers are familiar with the Jamaicans in the area and none of them have been identified as the perps."

"Captain," said Detective Buchanan, "we've brought photos of all our known Jamaican crime figures as you've requested. Our Captain said to inform you that if you need additional manpower from his department to give him a call."

"I will thank him personally for that offer, but at present, we have the manpower we need. What I really need from you and your department is your assistance in broadening the scope of this investigation and ultimately the search." He leaned over, hit the intercom button on his desk and asked his secretary to have Officer Anthony McCoy report to his office.

Sergeant Fuller turned onto East 91st Street and came to a full stop in front of a group of Jamaican men. At the same time four squad cars full of police officers came to a full stop surrounding the men, guns drawn. Lieutenant Fisher pulled his gun and ordered the group of men to lie flat on their stomachs. The six men complied with their hands spread away from their bodies. They didn't make any attempt to run as two of the uniformed officers searched them, one at a time, then signaled to the Lieutenant that they were all clean.

The Lieutenant ordered them all to their feet. "Gentlemen, this block and the entire neighborhood is now closed to all drug activity. Any of you caught out here loitering will be thrown in jail, and we will deliberately misplace your paperwork, so you'll stay in jail as long as possible. I want the gun that was stolen from my officer before this day is out or you men are out of business permanently!"

The Lieutenant and the rest of his department knew all of these men by sight and knew that none of them had been a part of the group that held up officer McCoy. Every one of the men had mug shots in the precinct and had been ruled out, but the Lieutenant also knew that these men knew everything that went on in their neighborhood.

"Sammy!" said the Lieutenant to one of the Jamaicans, "I don't want to burst your bubble, but my Captain is steaming hot that some of your Jamaican friends held up one of our officers last night and stole his service revolver."

"Lieutenant, me no know nothing 'bout dat, you know we no in a dem things deh."

"Sammy, I don't want to hear that bullshit. I don't expect you or your friends to come out and tell me you know who did it. But I do expect to get a phone call before the day is out telling me where to find my officer's gun and those punks who held him up. If not, all hell will break loose in this neighborhood, and you know I keep my word!" The Lieutenant turned and walked to his car without saying another word, and the five cars disappeared as quickly as they had arrived.

The men stood there dumbfounded for a moment, then picked up where they had left off in their conversation before they were so rudely interrupted by the police.

"Sammy, a none a de youth dem in a de neighborhood rob de beast boy," said Jah Mikes.

"Mek me tell unnu right now," said Sammy, who was the leader of these men and the biggest drug dealer in the neighborhood, "me wan' unnu find out a who rob de beast boy before de day done, and tell de man dem fi lock down de weed house dem fi de rest a de day."

"But boss, a nuff money we ago lose, we can't mek dem police boy deh tell we when an how we fi eat food."

"Right now me no in a nothing wid de police dem, me no need de unnecessary heat. Just shut down de bloodclot base dem and wait fi de heat fi blow over. And mek sure unnu find out a who come round yah an' disrespect we."

The men dispersed in different directions, and Sammy headed across the street to his stash house.

"Lieutenant," said Sergeant Fuller, "we should have locked up all of those motherfuckers and threatened to send their asses back to Jamaica. I'm sure at least one of them would have given us some information, rather than be deported."

The Lieutenant smiled. "Fuller, you're still a hard ass. Those guys have money; threatening them with deportation won't work. This is how I see it, they are businessmen. Illegal as it may be, they are still businessmen, and I can tell you this, they don't like being out of business for long. Let's give them a few hours, and if nothing happens we'll come down on them even harder."

A few minutes past noon Chuckie and Stepper pulled up in front of Dreaddy's house. Stepper exited the vehicle, approached the building and rang the doorbell to the second floor apartment. Chuckie remained in the driver's seat with the motor running. He kept a keen eye out for any sign of trouble and had his gun in his lap. Bushwick was a neighborhood in Brooklyn that both men liked, but they had to be on extra alert in this part of town. There were many Jamaican groups here that would have liked nothing more than to see them dead. And many of those men were just as deadly as they were. However, most of those men would much rather take on Chuckie or Stepper alone than take them on when they were together. Some had tried occasionally, but came up short and lost their lives. So the rest had learned from the mistakes of those few, and decided to take them on only when they were not together. Chuckie and Stepper had gotten wind of their plot, and always made it a point to be together whenever they visited Bushwick.

Some of the neighborhoods in Bushwick, mainly the area where the men now found themselves, could turn into a wild west scene in the blink of an eye, like something right out of the movies with bullets flying in all directions. Stepper and Chuckie were always extra careful in this part of town.

Dreaddy, one of their closest friends, had lived in

Bushwick since arriving in America from Jamaica in 1981. From the very beginning, he loved the neighborhood and the people. A week after he arrived he decided to scout out the neighborhood. He had walked a few blocks, just taking in the sights, when suddenly he came upon a dead body laying a bit off from the sidewalk in an open lot that was filled with overgrown weeds. He was sure the guy was dead so he kept walking. However, all that night and the next day he couldn't shake the thought from his mind that the guy may not be dead. The next day he walked back to where he saw the body and, to his amazement, it was still in the same spot and beginning to smell in the summer heat. It had to have been there for quite some time before he first saw it. He noticed people walking by on their way to work, covering their noses and minding their own business. The body remained in the lot for an entire week before someone finally called the police. Dreaddy fell in love with Bushwick and the people who lived there, and with that experience he knew right away that it was his kind of town.

Dreaddy peeped out through his upstairs window to see who was ringing his bell, and when he saw it was his boys, he opened the window and threw the front door key down to Stepper.

Chuckie killed the Volvo's ignition, got out of the vehicle and locked it. Stepper used the key to open the front door of the two family house as Chuckie joined him on the steps, then they made their way up the flight of stairs to Dreaddy's second floor apartment. Dreaddy was alone in the apartment preparing some fried fish for lunch. Marcia, his girlfriend, was out running errands.

"Yo! chef, me smell de food all de way out pon de street, I man check seh is a restaurant you have a run up yah. Me a tell you, you fi open a restaurant," said Stepper.

"A nuff boy would a love fi see me do dat, so de nigga dem can come creep up pon me when me back turn to dem 'bout me a cook food."

The men broke out in laughter.

"Yea, me can see you now, one hand a stir de pot and de next hand pon you gun to rawtid," said Chuckie.

"So wah unnu a do, unnu a chill out and eat some food?" asked Dreaddy.

"Yea man, me wi' eat two a dem fish deh," replied Stepper.

"Wah 'bout you Chuckie?" asked Dreaddy.

"Yea man, hook me up," replied Chuckie.

The men ate, smoked a few spliffs, and got down to business.

"Dreaddy, you nah go guess who me just see?" said Chuckie.

"Who you a talk 'bout?"

"Nuh de boy Roy, we catch de pussy a sleep in front a Club Jamaica Inn. Me paint de door wid de boy marrow."

"Nice move, a long time de nigga fi get pitch. Me well want catch him friend Mafia, me a tell you, any weh me catch him me a lick him down," said Dreaddy.

"Yea man, a now de pussy a go hide. But right now we deh pon a different mission. We wan' go check out a works weh Cow have fi we. Wah you a seh, you a mek de move wid we?" asked Stepper.

"Yea man, me wi' tek a ride, but me have a little works me well wan' tek, a long time me a size it up," replied Dreaddy.

"Yea, Chuckie a tell me seh you have a big works."

"Wait till unnu hear 'bout dah works yah. De boy Danny have a coke house in a basement apartment we a clock hard. Dem have a boy in deh weh a sell de crack and anytime de fool hear seh police deh pon de block him run out a de basement wid de money and de drugs fi go lock it off upstairs in a dem apartment pon de first floor. A deh so dem keep all a de money and de rest a drugs. All we haffi do is just go deh and tell de fool seh police a come and just wait fi him a de basement door. We can hold de boy and carry him go upstairs go clean dem out."

The three men laughed until tears came to their eyes.

"Wait deh," said Chuckie, "you mean to tell me, all we haffi do a tell de fool seh police a come an' him run out a de spot?"

"Yea man, me see it wid me own eyes."

"Yo! Me haffi see this fi me self. Wah you a seh Stepper?"

"It hard fi seh no to dat, it come in like taking candy from a baby to rawtid. Dreaddy, you still have de box a thirty-eight Special?"

"Yea, me have 'bout thirty a dem lef in a de box."

"Me just get a police boy gun last night, me want de teeth dem fi it, and bring de Mac-ten an' mek we circle de boy dem," said Stepper.

Dreaddy retrieved the box of thirty-eight bullets and the Mac-ten. He donned his bullet-proof vest and put on his army coat over it, tucking his nine millimeter Luger in his waistband and placing two spare clips into his coat pocket before the three of them left the apartment.

Lieutenant Fisher and Sergeant Fuller pulled into the

parking lot of the 71st Precinct, then made their way to the Captain's office. Lieutenant Fisher knocked on the door and the Captain told them to come in.

"Captain," said Lieutenant Fisher, "there was a homicide in front of Club Jamaica Inn on Rogers Avenue."

"Yes, I heard the call. Do you think there's any connection with our suspects?"

"It is too early to tell sir, but our victim appears to be a Jamaican male. The crime scene is being run by Detectives Majors and Williams. We have not yet positively identified the victim, and we have no witness to the shooting. The victim was hit twice and died on the spot. We've recovered a bullet that was lodged in the door frame of the club. I've instructed Detective Majors to forward any information they come up with on the victim as well as any ballistics information they get on the weapon."

"Good, and what about shaking that tree over in the 90s?"

"Fuller and I took care of it personally; I think it's just a matter of time before we get some results. I spoke to the big wig himself in that neighborhood, one Samuel Harrison," replied Lieutenant Fisher.

"Harrison... Harrison... I remember that name, we've had him in here a few times before haven't we?"

"Yea, he's the same one."

"Fisher, two detectives from the Special Crime Task Force are here. They're sharing their mug files with us. Officer McCoy is with them going through their books. I want both of you to work with them on this case."

The three men walked down the hall to a waiting room where Officer McCoy and the two detectives were going over the mug shots.

"Gentlemen," said the Captain, "this is Lieutenant Fisher and Sergeant Fuller, my leading officers on this case."

The detectives from Manhattan introduced themselves.

"McCoy," said the Captain, "any luck on finding any of those punks?"

"No Captain, I'm going through the last book right now."

Sergeant Fuller walked over to the desk and looked over Officer McCoy's shoulder.

"Stop right there McCoy!" said Fuller. "Lieutenant, take a look at this guy."

The Lieutenant walked over and took a close look at the picture in the album. "Damn Fuller, if it isn't our victim." The two detectives from the Special Crime Task Force walked over to take a look at the picture.

"That's Raymond Alphonso, a.k.a. 'Roy'," said Detective Buchanan.

"Do you have an address on him?" asked Lieutenant Fisher.

"We have a Queens address for him, I think it's his mother's address," replied Detective Buchanan.

"I want everything you have on that guy," said Captian McKenny.

"As I recall," said the other detective from the Task Force, "he is a part of a crime ring run by a Michael Brown a.k.a. 'Mackie'."

"Mackie!" said the Lieutenant, "if it's the same Mackie I'm thinking about, there'll be a lot more bodies in this city before the day is done. I have to give Detective Majors a call."

"I'd like to give my Captain a call and bring him up to speed on the turn of events with Roy," said Detective Buchanan.

"You can make the call in my office," said the Captain.

Chuckie, Stepper, and Dreaddy parked their vehicle around the block and made their way to the coke house on foot. They split up on their approach to the building, which was a dilapidated six-family unit with a side entrance to the basement. A staircase led directly from the basement to the first floor lobby. The neighborhood was somewhat deserted this time of day, only a few drug addicts could be seen going in and out of buildings, either to purchase their drugs or to get high. Everything else appeared normal as the men made their way to the building.

Dreaddy went in through the basement entrance followed by Chuckie and then Stepper. Chuckie and Stepper stood to the side of the basement entrance, out of sight of the guy who was selling the drugs, just in case he looked through the peephole in the door.

Dreaddy knocked on the door, and the guy looking through the peephole asked what he wanted. Dreaddy purchased two bottles of crack and then told the guy behind the door that two police squad cars were parked on the block. He quickly hid in the corner of the building where his two partners were waiting, and within a few seconds they heard the locks opening. A tall dark-skinned Jamaican guy emerged carrying a large shopping bag. The three men were on him before he could blink.

"Don't move pussy!" said Dreaddy.

The guy froze in his tracks, fear written all over his

face. Stepper snatched the bag from him as Chuckie frisked him. Stepper inspected the contents of the bag. In cash there was only about four hundred dollars, which was disappointing. Next to the money was a chrome Colt forty-five automatic, and a separate bag containing hundreds of crack vials ready for sale. The three quickly led the guy back into the basement apartment.

"Alright! Me no in a no games wid you pussy, weh de money deh?" asked Stepper.

"This a all de money me have, me just open up de base."

"Pussy, who and who upstairs in a de apartment?" asked Stepper.

"Danny, Rock, and him gyal."

"Alright, we ago walk you go upstairs, don't try nothing or you dead. Make sure you get dem fi open de door."

They led him up the staircase in the basement to the first floor lobby. The terrified man led them to the first floor apartment to the right of the front door entrance; there was one other apartment on the first floor. The men crouched on both sides of the man and Stepper knocked on the door.

"Who dat?" inquired the man behind the door.

"Bruce!" came the reply.

"A wah de bloodclot you a do upstairs so soon?" came the reply from the other side of the door as the locks clicked open. Suddenly the door swung wide and Dreaddy pushed Bruce with all his might into the man who had opened the door. They barged into the apartment with guns drawn behind Bruce. Danny, who had answered the door, had his nine millimeter cocked and ready and when Bruce was pushed into him the gun went off, hitting Bruce in the stomach. The forward motion of Bruce's body knocked Danny to the floor. Stepper rushed in, placed the Mac-ten square in Danny's face and relieved him of his gun. At the same time Dreaddy and Chuckie rushed past Stepper into the living room and caught Rock as he tried to leave through the living room window. Rock had thought it was a police raid and was in the process of making a quick exit. His girl was on the sofa, eyes wide and paralyzed from shock and fear.

"Don't move boy!" ordered Chuckie. "Move 'way from de window boy!"

Rock froze in his tracks and backed away slowly from the window. When the woman realized it was not the police, she began screaming from the top of her lungs.

"Shut you mouth bitch!" shouted Dreaddy.

The woman summoned her courage and suddenly went silent. The men knew they had to move fast because the shot was sure to have alerted the neighbors.

"Weh de money deh boy?" demanded Chuckie.

"No money no deh yah pussy!" replied Rock.

Chuckie was pissed. Without another word he pointed the gun in Rock's face and squeezed the trigger, killing him instantly.

Dreaddy went over to the woman and shot her in the head as well.

When Stepper heard the two shots, he removed the police special from his waistband, placed it on Danny's forehead and squeezed the trigger, then he stuck it under Bruce's chin and squeezed the trigger again; blood splattered the ceiling above him.

Chuckie and Dreaddy made a quick search of the apartment and found five thousand dollars and thousands of vials of crack. Before leaving they left some of the crack vials next to one of the bodies for the police to recover, and wiped down the doorknobs and locks of any fingerprints they may have left. They were always very careful, but opening and closing the front door was sure to leave a print or two so Stepper wiped the knobs clean before leaving the apartment.

Dreaddy rushed back into the basement apartment and retrieved the shopping bag of cocaine they had taken earlier from Bruce. He wiped down the doorknobs, then exited the building and headed straight to the vehicle as Stepper and Chuckie followed him on the opposite side of the street. Just as the men sat down in their vehicle, they heard the first of a series of sirens heading in their direction.

They got out of the neighborhood safely, but nothing was said. Things had not gone the way they had planned. There was no joyous moment during the ride, nor would there be any celebration over the events that had transpired.

As the men approached Dreaddy's apartment, Stepper broke the silence. "A wah happen in deh?"

"The boy rub me de wrong way and time did a run out in deh," replied Chuckie.

Stepper didn't like what happened but he knew Chuckie did the right thing. Bruce would have died anyway from the gunshot wound he received from Danny, and there was no way they could leave any eyewitnesses. Stepper reflected on the incident; four dead bodies, no big deal, the law don't give a fuck, just another drug deal gone bad.

Lieutenant Fisher sat in his office with the phone pressed against his ear. Detective Majors was on the other end of the line. Lieutenant Fisher was explaining to him the turn of events that led up to the identity of the shooting victim on Rogers Avenue.

"I just got a preliminary report on the bullets we recovered from the crime scene," said Detective Majors.

"What have you got?" asked Lieutenant Fisher.

"The one we took out of the door jam was in fairly good condition, it came from a thirty-eight special and can be traced. The other one though, was too damaged to run a match, but it was also fired from a thirty-eight. We didn't find any casings at the scene, which means it was fired from a revolver."

"I'm going to send you the ballistics report on officer McCoy's service weapon; I want you to run a test and get the results back to me as soon as possible," said Lieutenant Fisher.

"Will do, Lieutenant."

Back in the Captain's office the Lieutenant informed him that Roy was killed with a thirty-eight. "I have a feeling about this one Captain. Our suspects may have struck using Officer McCoy's weapon. Most Jamaican thugs are not in the habit of carrying thirty-eight revolvers; they like automatic weapons and magnums."

"Get McCoy's ballistics report over to Major's lab boys and see if there is a match," said Captian McKenny.

"I'm on top of it, sir." Lieutenant Fisher left the Captain's office and made the necessary arrangements to forward the ballistics report to Detective Majors.

Sammy sat in his stash house on East 92nd Street counting his money into one thousand dollar stacks. The doorbell rang and he quickly threw a beach towel over the money, then retrieved his nine millimeter as he made his way to the door.

"Who Dat?"

"Jah Mikes."

Sammy opened the door and let in his right-hand man. "Wah happen?"

"Yo! Remember de gyal Carol weh live pon Kings Highway?" asked Jah Mikes.

"Carol... Carol... yea me 'member de bitch. Wah 'bout her?"

"Come in like de boy Stepper a grind her off, de nigga did over her house Sunday night. Me check seh a him thief de police boy gun."

"How come me just a hear seh de boy a come 'bout yah still?"

"Me just a find out me self. Her friend name Gloria a show Larry seh de boy did over deh Sunday night."

"De gyal Gloria want a man gi' her one box in a her face and run her out a de area. De gyal should a mek man know seh de nigga a come 'bout yah long time ago," said Sammy.

"Yea, a true thing dat, but you know seh dem gyal deh just licky-licky, always a look something fi nothin' from some nigga. Sammy, mek we hold de gyal Carol and mek she call de nigga and lower him over her house, we can brush him once and for all."

"Come in like you nah think, if we lick him down right now, dat a go start a big war, and we can't afford dat wid de police dem a run wild. If we lick him down we have fi lick down him friend Chuckie, then we have de dutty boy Dreaddy and we have de boy Pops fi deal wid," said Sammy.

"But right now a we a catch hell fi dem anyway, it nah go mek no difference, de police boy dem done a blame we fi hold up dem boy, and dem know seh we no have nothin' fi do wid it. De boy Stepper and him friend dem totally disrespected I and I, we can't just sit back and mek dem get 'way wid dat, de nigga fi get a bullet fi that. De nigga know seh a we de police boy dem a go terrorize and de dutty boy still disrespect I and I. We haffi do something 'bout dat," said Jah Mikes, steaming hot.

"Right now de I fi just cool, a no we de police boy dem want, a dem, all we haffi do a mek dem tek care a dem," said Sammy.

Jah Mikes gave his friend a suspicious look; he could not believe what he was hearing from his boss. Was Sammy really thinking of turning in Stepper and his friends to the police? Jah Mikes didn't like it, but then, he thought, what the fuck, fuck dem. Better they suffer than he and his boys, but deep down he knew it wasn't right; he had no respect for anyone who worked with the police. He would never in a hundred years have figured that his boss would stoop that low. He had always looked up to him, but now it was clear to him that Sammy was intent on doing just that. Maybe he should reevaluate whether or not he could truly trust Sammy any longer and continue working with him. But he also knew that in this business one couldn't just quit, walk away and expect to live. For him to sever his ties he would have to kill Sammy or Sammy would kill him; that was the only way out of this mad game. Jah Mike's view of Sammy had now changed drastically; he lost all respect for him.

Chapter 4

The time was 2:00 p.m. and in less than three hours the men had committed five homicides. Chuckie, Stepper, and Dreaddy sat in Dreaddy's apartment, taken aback that all they got from the robbery was $5,400.

Chuckie poured out the bags containing thousands of vials of crack onto the carpet and counted them all. There were 9,000 vials of crack cocaine, with each vial selling for ten dollars, bringing the total value to $90,000. The men felt a little better knowing that the crack could be converted into a substantial amount of cash. However, they were no longer in the business of selling drugs, so they would have to pass it off to someone who could sell it for them. It was still a major haul, but with a slight setback as far as they were concerned, since they would have to wait for the drugs to be sold before they could get their money.

They were still angry thinking of the delay involved. They never thought of robbing for petty amounts, they always made it their duty to rob big. And when things didn't pan out for them the way they expected, as in this robbery, they got pissed off. They frequently left behind thousands of dollars worth of drugs from robberies, taking only the money. These outlaws shared the philosophy that when one takes the risk of stealing drugs, then one has to turn around and take a second risk, the risk of selling it. Given that belief, these men had always put all their energy and effort into stealing cold hard cash.

"Mek we tek a portion a de drugs go let off pon Cow a Flatbush and de rest we can let off pon Pops a Bronx, dem wi' get rid a it," said Stepper.

"Bushwick kind a hot right now, the best thing right now a fi just chill out yah so till it dark," said Dreaddy.

"Cho, fuck de police boy dem, mek we flash go a Flatbush, Cow a look fi we check him," said Stepper.

Chuckie chimed in. "Yea, mek we lef yah so, I no feel too right fi just a linger 'bout yah so."

The three men piled into Chuckie's Volvo and headed out of Bushwick. On the way to Flatbush they saw several police cruisers and a few ambulances heading in the direction of the crime scene. They felt at ease knowing they were heading out of the neighborhood before everything hit the fan. The police would be terrorizing every Jamaican group in the neighborhood before the end of the day, but they weren't worried; there had been no witnesses at the scene of the crime. Anyway, this crime would just be added to the long list of unsolved homicides in the state of New York. Crimes like this occurred every day.

They believed that they were soldiers fighting a war, and the killings were casualties of that war, pure and simple. What allowed them to sleep at night was knowing that the people they killed were killers just like them. They were all soldiers and, if given the chance, those men wouldn't hesitate to kill them just the same.

Sure, there were those who just happened to be in the wrong place at the wrong time, but the men didn't see them as being innocent people, they saw them as collaborators. There was no way they could be trusted not to identify these men in a lineup, so they too had to die in this terrible war. They became collateral damage.

Lieutenant Fisher was waiting in his office for the ballistics report from Detective Majors when the phone rang. "Yea, Lieutenant Fisher."

It was a woman's voice. "The man you are looking for goes by the name of Stepper." Then the phone went dead.

"Hello! Hello!" Lieutenant Fisher yelled into the receiver, then realized the line was dead. He wrote the name down on his notepad and sat there for a few seconds thinking long and hard about it, but nothing came to mind. He didn't think he had heard the name before. The phone rang again, and he grabbed it on the first ring. "Lieutenant Fisher!"

" Lieutenant Fisher this is Majors."

"Oh! Yea Majors."

"Lieutenant we have a positive match on the bullet, it was Officer McCoy's weapon that was used in that homicide."

"Bingo! I had a feeling it was. Majors, have you ever heard of a guy who goes by the name of Stepper?"

"Stepper... Stepper... I've heard it used before as a title but not as a person's name. It's the term Jamaicans use for most stickup thugs."

"Well, apparently there's a guy going by that name in Brooklyn. I want you to find out who the hell this guy is and where we can find him; he is now our prime suspect."

"I'll get on it right away. I'll start with Club Jamaica Inn, someone there may have heard of him." There was a pause, then an excited Majors said, "What? Lieutenant, Detective Williams just informed me that we have a quadruple homicide in Bushwick. I'm heading out there right now."

"Were they Jamaicans?" asked the Lieutenant.

"I don't know at this point."

"I'll meet you out there."

Chuckie, Stepper, and Dreaddy pulled up in front of Cow's apartment building on Ocean Avenue and hit the horn. A few seconds later Cow looked out through his fourth floor window. Stepper shouted, "Yo! Bad boy, wah you a say?"

"Everything cool, rope in!" replied Cow.

The men got out of the car and Chuckie opened the car trunk to remove a duffel bag containing the crack cocaine and the hand guns that were taken from the victims.

Cow buzzed the men in through the front door and they made their way up the four flights of stairs. Cow was at the front door of his apartment waiting for them. "Yo, me bredda, wah unnu a say?"

"Me deh yah, puppa," replied Chuckie.

Cow lived with his wife Barbara and three year old son who he affectionately called 'Junior Cow.' Barbara was at work and Cow was watching his son.

"Cow," said Stepper, "We just take off some food from a boy, me want you get rid a some coke fi we."

"How much a it unnu have?"

"We have 'bout nine thousand ten dollar bottles."

"Me no know if me can move so much a it, me we tek 2,000 a dem and gwaan work wid it, but me can't promise unnu how fast me wi' sell dem."

"That total twenty thousand dollars, we can split it four ways," said Stepper.

"We still wan' fi get rid a de rest a it, you know anybody weh wi' buy 'bout three thousand a dem?" asked Dreaddy.

"Me know some youth off a Flatbush Avenue, round a Twenty First Street weh might take de three thousand if de price right."

"You can gi' dem a check, and see wah dem a say. De four thousand weh lef me wan' let off pon Pops a Bronx," said Chuckie.

"Watch yah, me can't lef yah so right now till Barbara come from work and tek Junior Cow."

"Well watch yah, we ago lef five thousand a dem wid you then, just do wah you have fi do," said Chuckie.

"That wi' work, but how much me fi charge them a bottle?" asked Cow.

"Charge them six dollars a bottle, that a eighteen thousand dollars fi the three thousand. Take your cut and hold on to the rest a money fi we," replied Chuckie.

The men then got down to the main matter that brought them to Cow's apartment.

"So Cow, wah happen to de works you say you have fi we?" asked Stepper.

"Is a nice works, me would a tek it meself but de boy dem know me. De boy dem have a coke house we a clock hard, right off a Church Avenue. The apartment deh pon de second floor right over a store front weh boarded up. De window pon de coke house broke out next to de fire escape, all de man dem haffi do is climb up de fire escape and go through de window while de boy deh a de front door a sell de drugs. One a de man dem can go a de front door and keep de boy busy, while de rest a man dem can go through de window and creep up pon de boy. Is a easy works and de boy dem a make a bag a money in a dat spot deh."

"That sound nice, how much money you think them have in deh?" asked Dreaddy.

"A nuff money dem clock a day, but the thing is fi hold the boy and make him carry you go upstairs a de stash house, which a de apartment right above de crack spot."

Stepper thought back to the job they just pulled off a little over an hour before and smiled. Cow had no idea what Stepper was smiling about. Stepper glanced over to Chuckie and then over to Dreaddy and noticed that they were also smiling. It was clear that his two partners shared his sentiments. "So Cow, when we can make dah move deh?"

"De I them haffi wait till it get dark, so nobody no spot de I dem when unnu a climb up de fire escape."

"Alright, a little past 3:00 p.m. now, we ago flash go check Pops a Bronx and come back by about eight o'clock. By then you should a let off the three thousand bottles pon you boy dem a Twenty First Street," said Chuckie.

"Yea man, by dem time deh everything should a cool," replied Cow.

"Cow, we have a nine millimeter and a forty-five Colt we tek off a boy, which one a dem you want?" asked Stepper.

"Wah, mek me see dem!"

Stepper handed Cow the two automatics. The men

had decided to give one of the guns to Cow and the other to Pops before leaving Bushwick. Cow was one of their dearest friends. He was not considered an outlaw, he was a family man and the men tried their best to keep it that way. They knew they could trust him with their lives, but they still made it a point to keep him in the dark about the many things they had done and the incident in Bushwick would be another one of those dark secrets he would never hear of from them. Cow was very loyal to his friends, he had proven that to them on many occasions, but they still kept many things from him for his own good. However, Cow often heard, through secondhand information, of the many things his friends had done and felt privileged to be a close friend of theirs. From time to time he would ask Stepper about the things he had heard about, which Stepper would always deny, saying that people were always giving them credit for things they did not do. Cow never really fell for it, but he played along just the same. He knew his friends were just being protective of him. He often daydreamed of making moves with Stepper and the crew, even though it was quite clear to him that they would have none of it. Stepper was his closest friend of the bunch, and was his son's Godfather.

Pops on the other hand, was an outlaw and did partake in many missions with the crew, so he was privy to all the war reports. The men knew they would share the entire story with him about what took place in Bushwick and the killing of Roy. This type of exchange was how they kept each other abreast of friends and foes.

Cow held both guns in his hands, felt the weight of each of them, then looked them over carefully. One was a

Baretta nine millimeter and the other was a Colt forty-five automatic. Cow chose the Colt. "When I lick a guy, I want know seh him stay down."

The men laughed, knowing that Cow wouldn't hurt a fly. Furthermore, he didn't have to, not with friends like Chuckie, Stepper, Dreaddy, and Pops. If someone was to even breathe hard on Cow and he reported it to his friends, all hell would break loose.

"If Barbara could a hear you right now, you wouldn't get no pum-pum tonight," said Stepper.

"Wah you mean tonight, him wouldn't get none fi a week or more," said Chuckie. They all laughed.

Lieutenant Fisher and Sergeant Fuller pulled up in front of the crime scene in Bushwick. The two detectives from the Special Crime Task Force were already on the scene along with a few detectives from the Bushwick homicide squad. Fisher and Fuller went up to the first floor apartment where they were met by Detectives Majors and Williams.

"Lieutenant, it looks like a robbery homicide," said Detective Majors.

"Do you have any I.D. on the victims?"

"We have positively identified one of the victims, a Donovan Anderson, a.k.a. Danny. He's a known drug dealer in the neighborhood. He's Jamaican, and I suspect the rest of the victims are also Jamaicans."

The Lieutenant inspected the entire apartment and took a close look at each of the victims.

"Are you getting the full cooperation of the officers in Bushwick?' asked Sergeant Fuller.

"We have worked closely in the past; I know most of them," replied Detective Majors.

"I want a full report on my desk as soon as possible," said Lieutenant Fisher.

"Do we have any witness or witnesses to the shooting?" asked Sergeant Fuller.

"Not to the actual shooting, but some of the tenants did hear shots being fired. We've also discovered a crack outlet in the basement, alleged to be operated by the victims," said Det. Williams.

"I'd like to have a look at it," said Sergeant Fuller.

They made their way down to the basement where they were met by other officers and the Crime Lab technicians. Everything looked to be in order and they left the building and stood outside.

"Detective Majors," said Fisher. "I want you to get the ballistics reports on those victims right away. We need to stay on top of this one and see if there is any connection between this one and the one in front of Club Jamaica Inn."

"I'll get back to you as soon as I get anything."

"In the mean time I'll drop in on our friends in the 90s and see if I can get anything on this Stepper character. I want you and your partners," said Fisher, referring to the two detectives from Manhattan, "to take a trip down to Club Jamaica Inn and inquire if anyone down there ever heard of a guy who goes by the name of Stepper. He's a possible suspect in the assault on officer McCoy and he may very well have been the shooter in Roy's homicide. You can reach me on the radio if you get anything."

"We'll get on it, Lieutenant," said Detective Buchanan.

Sammy sat in his living room with his girlfriend,

Sonia, next to him. "You sure a de Lieutenant you get pon de phone?" asked Sammy.

"Yea, him say him name Lieutenant Fisher," replied Sonia.

"Alright, everything cool, mek dem deal wid de dutty boy Stepper, a hope dem kill de nigga."

Sonia had her reservations. She didn't like the idea of telling on anyone, she wasn't raised that way coming from the rough streets of Trench Town in Jamaica, but she knew if she didn't do what Sammy told her to do she would receive a serious beating. She sat there reflecting on how she had lost all respect for this man she loved. She was deep in thought when someone knocked on the door.

"Sonia, get de door," ordered Sammy, as he reached for his nine millimeter and aimed it at the front door.

"Who dat?" demanded Sonia.

"Jah Mikes!"

Sonia looked through the peephole, then unlocked the door to let Jah Mikes into the apartment.

"Sammy, Peter just call me and a tell me say Danny and Rock dem get lick down a Bushwick, everybody dead in a de apartment."

"Wah! How that happen?"

"We no know right now, it look like a dem get rob. You want see, last week Danny a tell me seh de boy Dreaddy did a buy nuff crack from dem back-to-back, me a tell Danny fi watch de boy and if him slip up fi lick a shot pon him. But him a tell me seh de boy a spend nuff money pon dem, and him no know nothing 'bout de upstairs apartment, him just go a de basement apartment a buy him crack and step, it look like de boy a use it."

"So you think say a dem do it?" asked Sammy.

"I no know but you know seh a so dem nigga deh move."

"Who and who get lick down on deh?" asked Sammy.

"Danny, Bruce, Rock and him gyal name May."

"Weh Peter did deh when all a dat a gwaan?"

"Him seh him just lef de spot and go check him baby mother and when him come back him see all kind a police and ambulance in front a de building. Then him get fi find out from some a de people dem in a de area wha' gwaan."

Sammy and Danny had been in business together for quite some time. They were good friends from their early days in Jamaica, so Sammy took the loss hard. This incident touched him deep down and he felt fear for the first time in his life which just made him all the more ticked off. "Yo, find out fi sure if a de boy do it, in fact, fuck that! Get de man dem together, we a go find de boy Dreaddy and him friend dem and kill every one a dem."

"I man agree wid that, but we can't go a Bushwick right now, it too hot."

"You right, just get in touch wid de man dem and tell dem fi oil up de gun dem."

Jah Mikes left the apartment and headed back to his base on East 91st Street. As he pulled up and parked in front of his building, Lieutenant Fisher and Sergeant Fuller pulled up next to him. They seemed to have come out of nowhere, trapping him in his vehicle.

Lieutenant Fisher placed his nine millimeter on the dashboard of the cruiser, then rolled down his window staring Jah Mikes straight in the eye. "I have one name for you; Stepper! Where do I find him?"

Jah Mikes was taken aback by the question. He was

no snitch and he wondered how the hell the Lieutenant had come up with that name so quickly. Then it clicked in his mind, *that damn Sammy.* "I don't know the guy, but I hear he has a girlfriend named Carol who lives on Kings Highway." Jah Mikes spit it out before he could catch himself.

"What's the Address on Kings Highway?" asked Lieutenant Fisher.

"I don't know the address but it's the yellow house near the dental office on the second floor."

"Stay off the streets!" said Lieutenant Fisher as they pulled away. Then he radioed in for the two detectives from Manhattan to meet him right away on Kings Highway.

Jah Mikes hurried up to his apartment. He felt like shit for giving the police that information, but he reassured himself that there was no way anyone would ever find out what he did. It would have to be a secret that he would take to his grave.

Lieutenant Fisher and Sergeant Fuller parked down the street from the yellow house on Kings Highway next to the dental office. Ten minutes later they spotted the two detectives arriving and Sergeant Fuller blinked his headlights. The detectives from the Special Crime Task Force parked and walked over to the car. Sergeant Fuller hit the latch to open the door for the detectives and they got in the back seat.

The Lieutenant turned around in his seat to face them. "Gentlemen, this is the home of the girlfriend of our prime suspect, Stepper. He could be in there; we don't want to take any chances. I want one of you to secure the rear of the house while the three of us go to the front door. We don't have a search warrant, but we are looking for a murder suspect so we have probable cause, but don't get carried away."

Sergeant Fuller got out of the vehicle and retrieved a shotgun from the trunk and they all approached the house. Detective Bradley secured the back of the building, as the Lieutenant and the other two men made their way to the front door. The second floor mailbox had the name Wilson on it, and the Lieutenant wrote it down and then rang the buzzer. Within a few seconds a young woman came to the door. "Yes, can I help you?"

"Is Carol Wilson home?" asked the Lieutenant

"Who am I speaking to?" asked Carol.

"Oh, I'm sorry Ma'am." He produced his badge. "I'm Lieutenant Fisher and I would like to speak to Carol Wilson."

"I'm Carol Wilson."

"May we come in?"

Carol opened the door and let the men into the first floor lobby.

"Ms. Wilson we have reason to believe that a murder suspect is held up in your apartment," said the Lieutenant as the other two detectives made their way up the stairs to her apartment.

"There's no one here with me."

"Please stay here with me, Ma'am."

Sergeant Fuller and Detective Buchanan went through the apartment one room at a time, but the apartment was empty. Fuller signaled to the Lieutenant that the apartment was clear, and Carol made her way back to her apartment with the Lieutenant in tow.

"Ms. Wilson, you are in a lot of trouble. We are looking for Stepper; where can we find him?"

"I don't know where he is, we don't have a steady relationship; we're just friends."

"When was the last time you saw him?"

"I haven't seen or heard from him in over two weeks."

He knew she was lying. He had to find a way to break her. "Do you have a picture of Stepper?"

Carol felt trapped and pressured to give them something. "Yes, I have a picture of the both of us taken some time ago."

"Okay, we'd like to borrow that picture and I would like you to come with me down to the station to answer a few more questions."

"But I didn't do anything, why do I have to come with you?"

"We are not charging you with anything, we just need to talk to you a bit further."

Carol dressed and left the apartment with the detectives.

Carol and the detectives entered the 71st Precinct.

"Ms. Wilson, Sergeant Fuller will escort you to his office," said the Lieutenant who then made his way to the Captain's office. He entered the Captain's office and gave him the latest update. The Captain ordered him to work around the clock to bring the case to a close with the arrest of Stepper. The Lieutenant assured him that he wouldn't rest until he brought the case to a speedy conclusion.

Chapter 5

Chuckie hit the Franklin Delanore Roosevelt Parkway, north, heading uptown. As he bobbed in and out of traffic, the stereo in the Volvo pumped out Tiger's latest reggae hit: "Tiger in de dance, what a bam, bam." Chuckie was an excellent driver; driving was his gift. He'd been tested and had come out on top every time. Both Stepper and Dreaddy knew that if they were caught up in a police chase, Chuckie was the man to have at the wheel.

Dreaddy lit up a large spliff and handed it to Stepper who sat next to Chuckie, then he rolled another one for himself and lit it. "Yo! Tiger wicked no rawtid."

"Yea man, a the wickedest deejay out a Jamaica right now," replied Stepper.

"Man, me no hear nobody wid a style like him," said Chuckie.

"Any time him come a New York and a gi' a show we haffi gi' him a check," said Dreaddy.

They weren't in the habit of going to shows and dances, they had far too many enemies. In the past, whenever they attended a dance or a stage show, someone always wound up getting shot or killed, so they made a conscious decision to avoid going to dances and shows, especially in New York. It wasn't out of fear of their enemies, it was because it wasn't possible to kill all of their enemies without having every law enforcement agency in America after them. From time to time, however, they did venture out of New York to Connecticut, Boston, or Philadelphia to catch a show or a dance where they felt more at ease and were less likely to run into an enemy.

"Dreaddy, wah you a talk 'bout go check Tiger out when him come a New York, come in like a slaughter you wan' go slaughter people," said Chuckie.

They all laughed, knowing it was out of the question to attend such a show in New York or New Jersey without getting into a shootout with their rivals.

"A wan' tell unnu something, if we no catch de boy Mafia by then, a dat deh show me ago look fi de boy," said Stepper.

"Yea man, dem boy deh nah miss a show like that," said Dreaddy.

"And the thing is this, dem pussy deh know say I and I nah go no show, so we a de last people de fool would a expect fi see deh."

"De I dem right, we wi' cross dat bridge when we come to it, but right now, a dollars we a look," said Chuckie.

"You know, a dat me love 'bout you, no care how much you wan' brush a boy, money come first," said Stepper, laughing.

Stepper and Dreaddy knew without a doubt that Chuckie wouldn't hesitate to kill Mafia, and if it came to it, he'd go out of his way to bring about that end. As far as the crew were concerned, Mafia was as good as dead already, it was just a matter of time.

Chuckie exited the Franklin Delanore Roosevelt Parkway and headed up 125th Street, in the direction of the West Side Highway. As they passed the Apollo Theater toward Broadway, Stepper said, "No yah so de Dominican boy Flaco have him crack base?"

"Yea, a right deh so pon de second floor, Apartment 2A, but dem place deh stay hot," replied Chuckie.

"Me wan' check him one a dem day yah."

They continued up 125th Street, then hit the West Side Highway heading north and hit the exit at the George Washington Bridge. Chuckie made his way to the Cross Bronx Express, and took it to the Gunn Hill Road exit.

It was 4:15 p.m. when the men pulled up to the curb in front of Pops' weed spot. One of Pops' workers was standing in front of the building. Chuckie recognized him. "Yo! Baller, weh Pops deh?"

Baller crossed the street and approached the vehicle. Leaning into the driver's side window he acknowledged the two strangers who accompanied Chuckie, then turned his attention to Chuckie. "You wan' see, Pops get shot up last night real bad, him in a de hospital right now. A wait I a wait pon a youth fi pay de boy dem weh do it a visit."

"How come nobody no call me and mek me know?"

"I man did well want get in touch wid you, but I no have de I number. Pops never gi' me you number."

"How him a do?" asked Stepper.

"I no know right now, I no hear nothing from him baby mother yet."

"Who in a de apartment upstairs?" asked Chuckie.

"Nobody no up deh right now, a just I deh 'bout."

"Alright, mek we go upstairs, I no want sit down out

yah, I and I dirty right now."

They got out of the vehicle. Chuckie went to the trunk to retrieve a duffel bag containing drugs and a few guns, and then they crossed the street and went into the building. They climbed the flight of stairs to the second floor apartment, led by Baller who unlocked the door and led the men into the apartment. This was the first time Dreaddy and Stepper had seen the apartment. Stepper observed the place carefully. To the left of the front door was a bedroom. There was nothing in this room but a set of dumbbells, a steel bar and a weight bench, clearly just a workout room. A few paces down from the weight room was the bathroom, and next to that was the kitchen. Next to the kitchen was a second bedroom which contained a bed and a few pieces of furniture. Facing that room was the living room where there was a sofa, a few chairs and a desk. The apartment was empty otherwise, but had been kept very neat and clean. It looked livable but it was used solely for selling drugs.

Chuckie handed Baller the duffel bag to secure it, then they got down to the business at hand.

"A who shoot Pops?" asked Stepper.

"A de boy Jolly and him friend dem from round a Webster Avenue," replied Baller.

"How bad him get shot?" asked Chuckie.

"I no know fi sure but him pick up more than one shot. I did a try fi call him gyal but I no get no answer all day."

"A wah happen between him and Jolly dem?" asked Stepper.

"Jolly front him five pound a weed, but the weed did mix wid bird seeds and it slow the place down. So Pops tell him say him nah pay him wah him did a ask fi it.

From dat dem kick off."

"So mek him never gi' back de boy him weed?" asked Dreaddy.

"De boy say him no want it back, him want him money. It come in like him did a punk man off, so Pops tell de boy him nah pay him fi nothing."

"Yo, me a tell Pops fi lef dem boy deh long time. Me a tek a ride go check him gyal. Dreaddy, chill out wid Baller till we come. Stepper tek a ride wid me," said Chuckie.

Chuckie made a u-turn on Gunn Hill Road and headed towards White Plains Road, which was about five or six blocks from Pops' weed spot. Once on White Plains Road they drove for about twenty blocks to 225th Street where Pops shared an apartment with his girlfriend. As Chuckie approached Pops' apartment building he spotted Pops' girl, Cherry. He hit his horn and called out to her. "Cherry!"

She immediately turned around, and when she recognized Chuckie she stopped in her tracks. She didn't recognize the other man in the vehicle, but assumed it must be Stepper. She had never met him before but she had heard many stories about him from Pops and other Jamaicans in the neighborhood.

Chuckie parked the car and both men walked over to Cherry, who led them to her building and up to her second floor apartment.

"Cherry, a me brethren Stepper this."

Cherry acknowledged him.

"How me brethren Pops a do?"

"It no look too good fi him, him get shot twice, one inna him belly and one inna him chest," replied Cherry, who broke down in tears. Chuckie held her and assured her everything would be all right, but in the back of her mind she felt it was already too late for him. "Me just come home fi take a shower and go back a de hospital, me deh deh from one o'clock this morning, me lef him mother deh wid him. Him come out a surgery a five o'clock this morning but him still pon critical list."

"Alright, see some money yah, take a cab go back a de hospital when you ready. If anything change call me beeper number, punch in twenty-two and me wi' know a you. Just call me anyway in a few hours and make me know something." Chuckie wrote out his beeper number on a piece of paper and handed it to her, then reached into his pocket for some money. He handed her five hundred dollars and told her to let him know if she needed more.

Stepper was visibly upset and hadn't said a word to her, but Cherry didn't view his behavior as disrespectful. From what Pops had told her about Stepper, she knew he had mad love for Pops and she could see that he was hurting deeply.

The men left the apartment. Stepper was pissed, and Chuckie knew it.

"Chuckie mek we tek a ride go around a de boy Jolly pon Webster Avenue. Mek Dreaddy gwaan hold down de fort till we come back."

Chuckie nodded, then made his way to the Cross Bronx heading to Webster Avenue. They were bent on revenge, no longer concerned with making money; it was blood they now craved.

As they drove by Jolly's building, they spotted one of Jolly's boys standing out front, a dreadlocks guy whose friends affectionately called him Ras Ruddy. It appeared that he was stationed there as a lookout, but he was being distracted by a pregnant woman. Ras Ruddy seemed to be deep in conversation with her and definitely sleeping on the job.

Chuckie parked the car up the street past the building without Ras Ruddy noticing them. Stepper got out and told Chuckie to wait in the vehicle. He held the thirty-eight police special down to his right side and walked slowly toward Ras Ruddy. It was broad daylight and the street was crowded, but Stepper didn't care, and no one saw him carrying the weapon in the open. People were too busy going about their business to take notice of the gun hanging by his side as he walked calmly toward his target. This was not the first time Stepper had displayed his weapon in this manner. He knew that most people, even if they saw the gun, wouldn't register the fact until it was too late. In most cases, those who happened to notice it would assume it was a toy or something other than a gun. Stepper eased his way up next to a white van right in front of Ras Ruddy, took careful aim, then shouted, "Dreadlocks!"

Ras Ruddy's eyes almost popped out of his head as he looked down the barrel of Stepper's gun, then, Boom! The deafening sound vibrated throughout the neighborhood, and those around seemed to freeze. The shot was the last thing Ras Ruddy heard as he fell back against the wall and then face down onto the pavement, the shot hitting him squarely in the forehead and splattering his brains onto the front door of the building. The pregnant woman Ras Ruddy was standing next to was expecting his child, and now his lifeless body lay on the ground at her feet. She instantly became hysterical, screaming at the top of her lungs as she realized what had just happened.

Stepper stood there looking at her, not showing any urgency in leaving the scene of the crime. In fact, he contemplated whether or not to kill her too.

The woman could not take her eyes off the weapon still in his hand, and even as she continued to scream, deep in the recesses of her mind she wondered why this man wasn't running away after gunning down her man in cold blood. Then suddenly, as if a light switch was flipped on in her mind, it became clear to her that he was going to kill her too.

Stepper leveled the gun at her stomach. She had a look of disbelief and dread on her face as Stepper gently pulled the trigger. Click. Nothing. The gun didn't fire. Stepper slowly turned and walked away from the woman, who had finally stopped screaming. He felt a sense of disbelief, but at the same time relief that the gun didn't fire. He didn't want to carry the guilt of killing a baby. Killing the woman, on the other hand, wouldn't have mattered to him at all. He would have killed her a thousand times over without a thought; she wouldn't have been the first woman he had killed, nor would she have been the last. A strange thought came to him as he made his way back to the vehicle, that God is real and surely had been with that woman and her unborn child.

Stepper and Chuckie sped off in the Volvo. Stepper chose not to mention to Chuckie what had happened with the woman and the gun not firing the second time, but he did tell him that Ras Ruddy was dead. Stepper held the thirty-eight in his hand and took a closer look at it. He opened up the cylinder, took out the spent shell, then he examined the remaining bullets in the cylinder. Sure enough, there was one with a dent in it, which must have occurred when the firing pin hit the bullet. That was clearly the one that didn't fire. He removed it from the cylinder and reloaded the entire cylinder with a fresh set of bullets.

By 6:30 in the evening Chuckie and Stepper had made their way to a smoke shop that Jolly owned off University Avenue. They parked a few doors away and walked back to the store. They entered the store and as they browsed around they noticed two men. Chuckie approached the older of the two. "Weh Jolly deh?"

The older man answered, "Jolly, no deh 'bout."

"Me wan' buy two pound a weed."

The man studied Chuckie's face intently and felt something wasn't right. Chuckie and Stepper seemed very suspicious to him, but something told him not to disrespect these men, and he couldn't bring himself to lie to them about not selling drugs because everyone in the neighborhood was well aware that the shop sold weed. He looked Chuckie straight in the eye and mustered up his friendliest and most non-offensive expression. "Me only have about half a pound right now but if you come back later me wi' have de--"

Before the man could finish the sentence Stepper pulled out the thirty-eight police special and leveled it at him. Chuckie pulled his nine millimeter and leveled it at the younger man who was standing less than a foot away. Chuckie and Stepper forced the two men to the back of the store.

"Weh de money and de weed deh?" demanded Chuckie.

The older man pointed to a suitcase in the corner of the room. Chuckie retrieved it and looked inside. There was about six pounds of weed in it and a few thousand dollars. Chuckie looked the older man straight in the eye. "How you say a half pound a weed you have?"

The older man said nothing with a look of defiance on his face and Chuckie hit him across his head with the gun. Blood ran down the man's face which was now covered in fear.

"Yo, listen to me right now, if you value you life and yuh friend life you better do wah me tell you. Me want you call Jolly and tell him say de weed run out and you have a customer deh yah right now weh want five pound a weed."

"Alright, me wi' call him but me a beg you no kill we," said the older man, whose body was now trembling.

"Calm down, a no you we want, we nah go do you nothing as long as you do wah we want," stated Stepper.

The man made the call and spoke to Jolly, whose greed got the better of him, even though he was somewhat reluctant because of what had just taken place with Ras Ruddy. Against his better judgment he told himself he didn't want to take a chance on losing a customer who had the money to buy five pounds, though he told the man at the store he couldn't believe that all of the weed was gone already and it wasn't even seven o'clock yet. The older man assured him he needed the weed right now, and Jolly's greed peaked again. The first ten pounds was sold and there was a possible sale for five more pounds! He told the man he'd be there in fifteen minutes with fifteen pounds.

Chuckie and Stepper tied up the two men in the back of the shop then locked the front door to the store.

Twenty minutes later Jolly approached the shop, accompanied by one his boys, each man carrying a shopping bag. Jolly noticed the shade was drawn over the

73

window of the door. "A wah de bloodclot Bobby a gwaan wid?" he said, to no one in particular as he eased out his nine millimeter and banged on the door.

Stepper unlocked the door and shot Jolly point-blank in his chest. The force of the impact knocked him backward, and the bag slipped from his grip as he managed to fire a reflex shot, aimed at no one. Jolly fell on his side a few feet from the doorway and onto the pavement. Although his sidekick was caught by surprise, he did get off a shot before Chuckie gunned him down and he fell face down on the ground. By this time Jolly had managed to get to his feet and was running down the block firing wildly as Stepper gave chase. Stepper took deliberate aim and fired, hitting Jolly in his neck, leaving a gaping hole below his chin. Somehow Jolly continued to move, but it looked like slow motion as he fell to one knee.

Stepper walked up and placed his gun directly on Jolly's head. "This a fi Pops!" He pulled the trigger and killed him instantly.

While Stepper was out chasing Jolly, Chuckie went to the back of the store and killed the men they had tied up. He left the store carrying the suitcase with the money and drugs, then picked up the two shopping bags Jolly and his sidekick had with them, and made his way to his car. Once in the Volvo, Chuckie raced down the street and picked up Stepper. They were off to regroup with Dreaddy and Baller.

The men had just killed Jolly and four of his boys out of utter vengeance for Pops' shooting. It was 7:30 p.m. and the number of homicides committed by these men had now climbed to ten.

Carol Wilson sat across the desk facing Sergeant Fuller when Lieutenant Fisher entered the room and spoke to her. "Ms. Wilson, Stepper is suspected of holding up a police officer and stealing his gun, and we want to speak to him about a homicide linked to that gun. I need you to tell me where I can find him before it is too late."

"Lieutenant, I would like to help you, but I don't know where to find him."

"You must have a phone number for him."

"He has never given me a phone number. Whenever I ask him, he tells me he don't have one."

"Ms. Wilson, you've stated that you haven't seen him in about two weeks or so, is that correct?"

"Yes, about two weeks."

"We have a serious problem with your story. We have a credible witness who states that Stepper was seen at your home as recently as yesterday. Before you say anything let me remind you, you can be charged with withholding evidence in a police investigation. Now I'm going to ask you again, did Stepper visit you yesterday at your home?"

"Yes, he was there," replied Carol, her voice trembling.

"Okay, what time did he leave your apartment?"

"It was probably about one in the morning."

"I need Stepper's full name and address."

"You may find it hard to believe but he has never told me his full name. Whenever I ask him, he laughs and tells me his full name is Stepper Stepper, so I just leave it at that. Our relationship, if you can call it that, is just about sex, nothing more, so I never pressed the issue."

"What kind of woman are you, sleeping with a man

whose name you don't even know? Alright, give me the names of some of his friends."

"I only know the name of one of his friends, a guy name Chuckie. I saw him once or twice before."

"Do you have a last name for him?"

"No."

"What kind of car does Stepper drive?"

"A black BMW."

"What kind of car does Chuckie drive?"

"I don't know. When I met him he wasn't driving."

"Sergeant," said the Lieutenant, "have Ms. Wilson go through our mug shots and see if she can pick out a picture of Stepper or this Chuckie guy."

"Will do," said the Sergeant as he left the room to retrieve the mug shot books containing pictures of every Jamaican who had ever been picked up in Brooklyn by the police department.

"Ms. Wilson, I'm going to level with you. You are in a lot of trouble if you do not help us find Stepper. We can charge you with, not only withholding information, but also with harboring a fugitive from justice. Both of these charges are very serious."

"Lieutenant, I didn't do anything wrong and I am trying to help you."

"Ms. Wilson, my Captain is pissed off and he wants to bring charges against you. I told him you are helping us, but if I don't get a name for him, he will come down on you very hard."

Carol was scared out of her wits. She couldn't see herself being locked up in a cell for even one minute, and she sure as hell wasn't going to risk that by protecting Stepper or Chuckie. For almost an hour she went through the books, but to no avail, there were no pictures of either

Stepper or Chuckie.

The Lieutenant was pissed. He felt Carol was protecting these men; he found it hard to believe that she didn't know any of their names or whereabouts.

"Sergeant, bring those mug shots that our boys brought in from Manhattan."

The Sergeant left the room then returned with two books. Carol was going through the last book when she came upon a photo and she called out to the Lieutenant. "That's Chuckie!"

The Lieutenant rushed over so fast he didn't notice a chair in his path. He bumped his foot on the chair leg, tripped and almost fell. He grabbed the desk for support and then regained his composure. He looked over Carol's shoulder at the picture, then read the name below it, Errol Palmer.

"Bingo! We have a New Jersey address on him. It says he lives with his mother," said the Lieutenant. "Sergeant, tell Detective Buchanan I want to see him right away. I want you two to take a trip to New Jersey and speak to this guy Chuckie."

The Sergeant rushed out of the room as the phone rang. The Lieutenant picked it up. "Fisher here."

"Lieutenant this is Detective Majors."

"Yea, Majors, what is it?"

"Lieutenant, you won't believe this, but we have a match in the massacre in Bushwick. Two of the victims were shot with Officer McCoy's service revolver."

"That son-of-a-bitch! He's on a killing spree in our city with our own gun."

"Three other guns were also used in the killings, so our boy has company."

"Okay, Majors, I have another name for you,

Chuckie, a.k.a. Errol Palmer; he's Jamaican. At this point he's just a material witness. I want you to run his name through Albany and see if anything comes up on him in New York. The only address we have on him is his mother's address in New Jersey, a Mrs. Campbell. I'm sending Fuller and Buchanan out to New Jersey to have a talk with him and see if he will volunteer to return to New York with them. In the mean time, I'm forwarding you a mug shot of Chuckie. I want you to show it around to the people at Club Jamaica Inn and see if anyone recognizes him."

"Will do, Lieutenant."

Detective Buchanan entered the office along with Sergeant Fuller. The Lieutenant asked a female officer to escort Ms. Wilson to another room before addressing the detectives.

"Gentlemen, we have a ballistics match on the homicides in Bushwick. Officer McCoy's gun was used to kill two of the victims in that homicide. There were three other weapons involved in those killings. We have to get those guys before anyone else is killed. Buchanan, we have a positive I.D. on one of Stepper's friends. Our witness picked him out from one of your mug shots: Chuckie, a.k.a. Errol Palmer. He is not a suspect at this time, but we need to speak to him. We have an address for him in New Jersey, where it says he lives with his mother, Mrs. Campbell. I want you and Sergeant Fuller to work together on this. Take a trip to New Jersey and question him personally."

Detective Buchanan picked up the picture of Chuckie to get a closer look. "Lieutenant, if I'm not mistaken, there's an arrest warrant out for this guy on a gun charge.

That gun, I think it was a forty-five automatic, was linked to a homicide that took place in Queens a year ago. To the best of my knowledge Errol Palmer is on the lam. I'll give my Captain a call and fill him in, and I'll see if we have anything else on him in our files."

"Well that changes everything. This Chuckie guy has now moved up to being a possible suspect in the Bushwick and Rogers Avenue homicides; he better have an airtight alibi. Sergeant, place an all-points bulletin out for his arrest. Also, call the Irvington Police Department in New Jersey and ask for their assistance in apprehending the suspect, and let them know you are en route."

"Yes, Sir."

Chuckie and Stepper hit the Cross Bronx Express Way, heading back to Pops' weed spot. Suddenly Chuckie's beeper went off and when he checked the code it read 22, the code he had given to Cherry to contact him. Chuckie handed the beeper to Stepper and asked him to write down the phone number. Chuckie took the first exit he came to and found a pay phone. He placed a call to the number and Cherry's tearful voice came over the line.

"Cherry wah happen?" asked Chuckie.

"Pops dead Chuckie! Pops dead!"

Tears ran down Chuckie's cheeks as Stepper watched him. He stepped out of the car and asked, "Wah happen?"

"Pops gone."

Stepper turned on his heels and went back to the car without saying a word; he needed a few minutes to grieve alone.

Chuckie regained his composure and continued speaking to Cherry. "Cherry, a seven forty-five now, wah time you wi' get home?"

"Me nah go back a de house tonight, me ago stay wid Pop's mother tonight."

"That's a good idea, give me a beep tomorrow and me wi' come see you."

"Alright," replied Cherry, then the phone went dead.

Chuckie returned to the car and hammered out his rage and frustration on the steering wheel. He started the motor and drove off to pick up Dreaddy. For a while the men rode in silence, and then Stepper put in a Bob Marley cassette. The music played, "Three little birds, sat on my doorstep."

Chapter 6

At 8:00 p.m. Chuckie and Stepper sat in a daze across the street from Pops' weed house. Each was lost in his own thoughts as customers made their way in and out of the building.

Stepper reflected on the day he first met Pops. He had been in Ronie Bops' Restaurant on Bronxwood Avenue ordering food to take back to a girl he was visiting in the Bronx. It was a beautiful summer evening, and people were out and about taking advantage of the cool evening breeze. After making his purchase he was heading back to the girl's apartment with his order in hand when he noticed two guys with knives drawn surrounding Pops, and it was clear that they were trying to kill him. But what really caught Stepper's attention more than anything else was the fact that there was no fear in Pops; he made no attempt to elude his two would-be assailants. Instead, he was calling them every name in the book, telling them that they were pussies and that they couldn't do anything to him. Stepper liked what he saw in young Pops right off because it reminded him of himself. Pops continued berating the two assailants when one of them seemed to lose control of himself and charged at Pops. He held his

knife high, aiming for Pops' head. Pops quickly raised
his right hand and blocked the advancing blow, then with
lightening speed he caught the guy with a left hook
square on the chin. The guy instantly dropped the knife,
fell to his knees and went face down, out cold. Stepper
was so impressed that he did something he vowed never
to do, intervene in someone else's business. Sensing that
the second guy was about to make his move on Pops
from behind, Stepper reached for his nine millimeter and
told the guy to drop the knife. The guy stopped dead in
his tracks just as he was about to make his move towards
Pops. The knife dropped from his hand and he started to
say something when Stepper cut him off abruptly. "Pick
up you friend an' leave the area!"

The guy was more than happy to comply. His friend
was just coming out of his concussion, so he helped him
to his feet and the two of them scurried away down
Bronxwood Avenue. When they were sure they were a
safe distance away from Stepper and Pops, they turned
around and called them every dirty name imaginable.

Stepper smiled and turned to Pops. "Real bad guys
aren't they?" They both laughed and Stepper introduced
himself to Pops. From that day on, Stepper took Pops
under his wing and taught him the ins and outs of making
money by the gun.

Chuckie was also reminiscing about the day he met
Pops. His mind drifted back to the day Stepper brought
Pops to Brooklyn and introduced them. It was a rainy day
in mid-summer and he hadn't been in the best of moods.
Chuckie didn't immediately take to the youth, but Pops'
personality grew on him quickly, and it wasn't long
before Chuckie started referring to him as his younger
brother. Even Dawn, Chuckie's woman, took a liking to

him and referred to him as her little brother as well. Thinking of Dawn suddenly brought Chuckie back to the present moment and he broke the silence in the vehicle. "Damn! Dawn no know say Pops dead. Yo, mek we carry de weed go in go lock off."

The men got out of the vehicle and went into the building. Dreaddy, who was stationed in the apartment's window overlooking the street had spotted the men when they first drove up. He kept a visual on them with his gun in hand, making sure they were safe. He held his place at the window until his two friends entered the building, then made his way to the apartment's front door where he waited for them.

As Chuckie and Stepper approached the apartment door it swung open and Dreaddy greeted them. "Yo, wah unnu a say?"

The men didn't respond, they just walked past him, the expressions on their faces said it all. Dreaddy knew right away that something had gone wrong, but he didn't press the issue, he just closed the door and followed them to the living room. Baller was in the apartment along with Rohan, Pops' other worker.

"A who dah youth yah?" asked Stepper.

"A Rohan this, him hustle with me and Pops," replied Baller.

Chuckie acknowledged him. "Yea, Pops did a show I 'bout him." Chuckie remembered seeing him before on a few occasions, but had never spoken to him. Baller was the only one of Pops' workers that Chuckie had ever dealt with. Chuckie wasn't in the habit of making friends very easily, nor were Stepper or Dreaddy. A person had to prove himself rigorously before any of these men would call him a friend.

Rohan had heard many stories about these three men and now he stood in their presence. Finally meeting them up close and personal, he was in awe. He recalled seeing Chuckie on two different occasions, though he'd never spoken to him. He knew these men were well respected and feared by many people. He looked up to them and would do anything to be accepted by them.

"How Pops?" asked Dreaddy.

"Him gone," replied Stepper.

Dreaddy became extremely agitated. "What! Yo, we haffi go draw down pon Jolly dem tonight, all a dem pussy deh fi dead!"

Chuckie pulled Dreaddy to one side of the room and motioned for Baller to join them. Chuckie led the two men into an adjacent room; he didn't want to speak openly in front of Rohan, not knowing him that well. He needed privacy in order to fill the men in on what had just transpired between him and Stepper, and Jolly and his crew.

Stepper knew what Chuckie was up to; the men had to be told. There was no reason for him to be in the room with them, so he stayed in the living room and kept Rohan company. Stepper knew that if Rohan was a part of Pops' crew he could be trusted, but these men were very cautious, and unwilling to share certain information with just anyone. Rohan would still have to prove himself before he would be trusted with this kind of information. Then, and only then, would he be included in the game of murder and its discussions. The men felt more at ease discussing such matters with Baller, on the other hand, because they knew that he had pulled the trigger on many occasions while in the company of Pops. Chuckie was well aware that Baller had been pulling the trigger from his Waterhouse days in Jamaica, where he and Pops had been friends since childhood. In New York, Baller and Pops had been kicking up hell in the Bronx for a long time. Yes, Chuckie thought, while sizing up Baller, Pops had trained him well; maybe one day he could fill the void left by Pops.

Dreaddy brought Chuckie out of his drifting state of mind. "So wah happen, Chuckie?"

"We just brush de boy Jolly and four a him boy dem."

"Yea man, Pops would a love dat, dem boy deh should a know say I and I play fi keeps."

Baller had a big grin on his face. "Me sorry me neva deh deh."

Chuckie put his right hand on Baller's shoulder. He liked the youth and he could see in his eyes that he meant it. "We take twenty-one pound a weed from de boy dem, and a few thousand dollars. We wan' gi' de money to Pops baby mother."

"Yea man, we haffi make sure she alright, she a one a we," said Dreaddy.

"Me ago mek sure she and the baby have everything dem need," said Baller.

Chuckie and Dreaddy had the utmost respect for Baller and knew he was sincere. He was not a selfish youth at all. Pops had always spoken highly of him to Chuckie, saying that he always put the people he loved before himself, but at the same time, he was the last person you would want to double cross.

Chuckie turned to Dreaddy and placed his hand on his shoulder. "A three a we now, we haffi take good care a each other." Chuckie chose his words carefully to maximize their effect on Baller and he thought it worked, however, there was no way to know for certain.

Dreaddy smiled, understanding what his friend was attempting. "No bother get soft pon me now."

Chuckie smiled at him.

The three men rejoined Stepper and Rohan in the living room. Stepper had all the weed spread out on the floor, twenty-one individual packages, each weighing a pound. "Rohan, which part a yard you come from?" asked Stepper.

"Me come from off a de Waltham, a thirteen."

"Yea, which part a de Waltham?"

"Fitzgerald Avenue."

Chuckie joined the conversation. "A which part a Waltham that deh?"

"Right a de burn out Post Office Building, down from Chiney Cemetery."

They all knew exactly where it was but they wanted the youth to talk so they could see where his head was at.

"You ever hear 'bout Ranch Man dem?" asked Stepper.

"Me know me hear dah name deh before, but me can't remember fully."

Stepper laughed. "That a before you time my youth."

"Me know 'bout Spade Gang dem."

"Yea, wah dem did name before dem name Spade?"

"Pigeon Gang!" replied Rohan with a smile.

Stepper smiled. He knew Rohan knew they were feeling him out. "A I turf dat, but when I deh deh you either was a baby or never born yet. You hear 'bout the police boy weh get lick down earlier this year a Far Rockaway?"

"Yea, me hear a Yard youth do it."

"A Ranch Man dat, a me brethren Dapper lick-down

de police boy. A Fitzgerald Avenue him come from, him mother name Miss Carmen. A him single-handedly mek all a de police dem a New York a go stop carry thirty-eights and a go start carrying nine millimeters," said Stepper.

"Me never know dat."

"Yea man, him and de police boy get in a shootout, Dapper have a nine millimeter and de police boy have a thirty-eight. De police boy empty him gun and a reload when Dapper ease up pon him and lick a shot in a de boy head. I man love him fi dat, because dem police boy deh kill nuff black youth in a cold blood."

"Me no like no police, dem kill me father when me did a five years old," said Rohan.

"Wah! Me feel it fi know dat. Right now we have every reason fi proud a de youth dem from thirteen, we no play wid police boy, we brush de pussy dem."

"Alright, enough a de bad man talk," said Chuckie, and the apartment filled with laughter.

Rohan was more at ease and instantly felt a strong liking for these men. "Me feel 'a way' 'bout wah happen to Pops, me ago lick down everyone a dem boy deh weh kill him."

The men looked at Rohan for a few seconds without responding, then Stepper spoke up. "You a my homeboy, mek me tell you something, you see we yah so, we love Pops, dem boy deh weh kill Pops bite off more than dem can chew, just cool and hold down de fort with Baller and leave the dirty work to I and I."

Rohan nodded, understanding that these men would avenge Pops' killing, though he didn't quite understand why they were so at ease. What he didn't know was that Jolly and four of his men were already laying in the city morgue and he'd be reading about it the following day in the New York Post.

Chuckie, Stepper and Dreaddy had to make some serious decisions that they knew would lead to a few changes in their lives. None of them had any interest in having a drug spot, but now it was evident to all of them that they were stuck with one. In a strange way, each of them felt they had to keep this weed spot going in memory of their fallen comrade.

"Wah we ago do 'bout Cow?" asked Dreaddy.

"Rawtid, we have fi gi' him a check, me know him a wait fi hear something from we right now. If anything, we have fi put off de works fi another day," said Stepper.

"So wah we ago do 'bout de four thousand bottle a crack we have?"

"We can gi' Flaco a check a Harlem and see if him wi' tek it off a we."

"Yea man, is a good idea dat. Me get de next Mac-ten from Baller weh Pops did have on yah, plus de bulletproof vest weh Pops did have."

"A pity him neva have it on when dem boy deh draw down pon him," said Stepper.

"Alright, Baller, hear wah me wan' you fi do, keep six pound a de weed on yah, and gi' Cherry de fifteen weh lef so she can hold on to it. Me ago gi' you five thousand dollars fi gi' her wid it. Tell her de money a fi her but de weed me want her fi keep fi we. Just tell her say you no wan' keep too much weed in a de spot in case de police raid yah. Call her tomorrow and set it up, she a stay a Pops' mother house tonight so she might no get back a de house till late tomorrow. Right now, me wan' you and Rohan gwaan run de spot. I and I wi' check in pon you as much as possible. Hold dah beeper number yah, punch in eighty-eight as you code number, dat way I wi' know a you when you call. Dreaddy, gi' de vest to Baller, and gi' him de nine millimeter weh we did have fi Pops," said Chuckie.

Dreaddy gave Baller the bulletproof vest, then went to his bag and came back with the nine millimeter and handed it to him. The men armed the two Mac-tens and placed them in the duffel bag along with the four thousand vials of crack. They bid their farewells to Baller and Rohan then left the apartment one at a time with Chuckie leading the way.

It was 9:15 p.m. and Chuckie was doing some serious driving. To make up for lost time, he hit the West Side Highway heading to Harlem.

Lieutenant Fisher sat in Captian McKenny's office. They released Carol Wilson, warning her not to leave town. They ordered a team of detectives to keep a close watch on her, and they obtained a Judge's injunction to place a tap on her phone.

"Captain, we have to get that guy; he has no regard for the law."

"I couldn't agree with you more, but we still don't have an address for him. I think our best bet is to keep a close eye on Ms. Wilson. I don't believe she was totally honest with us. I think she's trying to protect this Stepper guy."

"I feel the same way, she seems to be very fearful of the guy; I can't say I blame her, he is extremely dangerous," said the Lieutenant.

"Has the tap been placed on her phone yet?"

"Yes, everything is in place."

"Okay, all we can do is to wait for something to break. We will get them, we always do," said the Captain as his phone rang. "Yes, Captain McKenny."

"Captain this is Sergeant Fuller."

"Yes Sergeant, did you speak to Mrs. Campbell?"

"Yes sir, she has no idea of the whereabouts of her son, Chuckie. She said she hasn't seen or heard from him in over a month. She said that he sometimes stays with a girl in Brooklyn by the name of Dawn, but she doesn't know Dawn's last name or her address. She said Chuckie drives a 1986 brown Volvo, but she doesn't know the license plate number on the vehicle. I have the Irvington Police Department checking their motor vehicle records for a plate number in his name. I should have that information soon. Mrs. Campbell also gave us a name and a photo which may possibly be Stepper, A.K.A., Albert Roberts. She said he's been Chuckie's best friend for a number of years, but she doesn't know him as Stepper. She further stated that Albert Roberts is from New Jersey, and his mother and father still live there. I'm in the process of running a check on that name while I'm here to see if I can come up with anything on him as well as an address."

"Good job Sergeant, I will also run a check on that name in New York and with the F.B.I. to see if anything comes up. I want you and Buchanan back here as soon as you wind up everything on that end."

"Will do Captain."

Carol sat in her living room with a thousand thoughts racing through her mind. She was upset with Stepper for bringing this on her and at the same time she felt awful for giving in to the pressure from the police. She was never fond of the police since her early childhood in Jamaica. She had witnessed far too many shootings involving the police, and it seemed that they were never held accountable for their actions. She felt a renewed sense of bitterness towards them now. In her mind she ran through the different possibilities of how she could get word to Stepper before the police caught up to him, but nothing came to mind. She would just have to wait and hope to hear from him before it was too late.

Chapter 7

Chuckie made a right turn onto 125th Street then continued across Broadway Avenue, then to St. Nicholas Avenue. He slowed as he came parallel to Flaco's building; everything looked in order so he made a left and parked on Lennox Avenue. "Yo, Dreaddy, chill out with de car and mek me and Stepper go check Flaco, him get uncomfortable when him see too much people in front a him door."

"Yea man, me wi' gwaan jam."

Chuckie and Stepper took the drugs and walked up 125th Street towards Flaco's building. They entered the building and were climbing the steps to the second floor apartment when Chuckie suddenly froze and grabbed his neck. "Rawtid! Is like a man just crick me neck." He held his chain as fear gripped him.

Stepper had never seen fear in his friend's eyes before and it didn't sit well with him. "A wah happen to you?" he asked.

"De Cuban woman tell me say anytime me inna danger de chain wi' mek me know, me a tell you, de chain just crick me neck, a de first time that ever happen since me have de chain."

"You and dat damn Voodoo chain. Mek we do wah we haffi do so we can flash go a Brooklyn go check Cow."

Every fiber in Chuckie's body told him to turn around and leave the building, but before he could make his mind up, Stepper walked past him and was already on the second floor landing in front of Flaco's door, ringing the bell. Chuckie was on edge and not taking any chances; he made his way up the remaining steps, removed his gun from his waistband and stood to the side of the door.

Stepper stood in front of the door while Chuckie stood out of view. The door swung open to reveal a Spanish guy who Stepper didn't remember ever seeing before. "Weh Flaco deh?"

"Yea, he in de back, come on in."

The guy didn't see Chuckie, and as Stepper walked past him to enter the apartment, he put a gun in Stepper's back. "Don't move nigga!" He snatched the bag from Stepper's hand.

Chuckie spotted the move and before the guy could kick the door closed, Chuckie placed his gun at the guy's head and squeezed the trigger. He fell dead on the spot, without ever knowing what hit him. Stepper was covered in the dead man's blood.

All hell broke loose then and the apartment lit up with gunfire coming from the back room. Stepper and Chuckie fell flat on the floor and returned fire, but they had to figure out a way to get out of there before the police arrived. As Stepper kept up a heavy volley of shots at the men in the back room, Chuckie managed to back his way out of the apartment and position himself at the doorpost in the hallway. From there he let loose a barrage of shots as cover for Stepper who also worked his way out of the apartment crawling backwards. They escaped the building, but had to leave the four thousand vials of crack on the floor of the apartment.

Police sirens sounded from every direction as they returned to the car. Dreaddy saw the blood on Stepper and thought he was hit, but he managed to keep his cool as they fled. Chuckie quickly took his place behind the wheel and put the car in drive. He made the first right turn he came to and then to the Franklin Delanore Roosevelt Parkway, safely headed towards Brooklyn.

"Yo! Stepper, you get hit?" asked Chuckie.

"No, me alright, it look like you chain save we tonight."

Chuckie didn't respond.

"A wah happen back deh?" asked Dreaddy.

"It look like we walk in pon some boy weh did a rob Flaco, de boy try fi stick me up as me step through de door, but Chuckie lick him down, de fool neva see Chuckie, him think say a did me one deh a de door. Me haffi empty two magazines and empty the thirty-eight in deh before we get out. De boy dem did a fire a barrage a shot after we," replied Stepper, still hyped. "Rawtid, we did haffi lef all a de drugs in deh pon de floor, we couldn't get to it."

"Me brethren, dem thing deh come and go, the main thing is that de I them alright," said Dreaddy.

Chuckie remained quiet and deep in thought. Stepper looked at him and said seriously, "Chuckie, de I was in rare form back deh, I man wouldn't deh yah right now if it wasn't fi you. Mek me ask you something."

"Wah Dat?"

"How much me can get one a dem rawtid chain deh fa?"

The car erupted in laughter which brought Chuckie back to his old self. He hit the gas pedal and danced in and out of traffic with a big grin on his face.

They exited the Brooklyn Bridge, hit Atlantic Avenue to Flatbush Avenue, and then made their way to Ocean Avenue. At 10:20 p.m. they pulled up in front of Cow's apartment.

"Yo, me wan' we put off de works yah till tomorrow," said Chuckie.

"Well, we still haffi check Cow now that we deh yah," replied Stepper.

"Mek we see wah him a say, if anything, me one wi' tek de works," said Dreaddy.

Chuckie hit the horn and Cow acknowledged them from the window. They parked the car and went into the building. Cow buzzed them in and when they got to the door Stepper had his coat in his hands with the blood stains on it. It was his intent to wash it while in Cow's apartment.

Cow greeted them at the door. "Wah unnu a say, me deh yah a wait pon unnu all night."

"Nuff things a gwaan me brother," replied Chuckie.

The men entered the apartment and sat in the living room. Cow's girlfriend and son were already in bed, so they had some privacy and were able to speak freely.

"You want see, Pops dead," said Chuckie.

"Wah! How him dead?" asked Cow.

"Some pussy lick him down a Bronx."

"Mek we flash go pay them a visit."

"That done taken care of," replied Stepper.

"I man still vex, unnu know I check fi Pops, I haffi go lick down something fi him," said Cow.

"Right now the I fi chill, I and I no want de I get

95

hot," said Chuckie.

"Me nah worry 'bout dat, a pussy kill I brethren, I haffi do a pussy something."

"But we done tell you that taken care of, no body no lef fi kill," stated Stepper.

"Damn, unnu couldn't leave one a dem fi me?"

The men had to laugh.

"You no ready fi that yet Cow, chances are you would a vomit if you see a dead body," said Dreaddy.

"You can believe that if you want to," countered Cow.

"Cow, me wan' use de bathroom, me haffi wash me jacket," said Stepper as he got up and found his way to the bathroom.

"Cow lend me you phone, me wan' call Dawn and show her 'bout Pops." Chuckie dialed his house and Dawn answered the phone.

"Yea!"

"Dawn, wah happen?" asked Chuckie.

"No nothing, me a keep you food warm. Everything alright with you?"

"Yea, me cool but Pops dead."

"Wah! You a lie," said Dawn.

"Me deh a Bronx all day to rawtid, some pussy lick him down over some weed, him dead inna de hospital."

Dawn began to cry, so Chuckie knew it hit her hard; she was never one to cry easily.

"Weh you deh now, and when you a come home?" asked Dawn.

"Me deh over Cow, me soon reach on deh."

"Alright, me a wait up fi you."

Chuckie hung up the phone as his beeper went off.

At 10:00 p.m. a squad of men, accompanied by a woman, were out for revenge. Mackie and Mafia, along with a pair of notorious killers recently imported from Jamaica by Mackie, were out for blood. The imports were a male and a female team, known in Jamaica for killing police officers and gangsters. Many of those killings had been ordered by Mackie. The man was called Wakki and the woman was Obeyah.

Ann Marie was in her bed watching television when she heard a knock on her door, "Who dat?"

"A me Pearl," came the reply.

"Which Pearl dat, me no know no Pearl?"

"A Chuckie send me come bring something fi you."

"Hold on me a come." Ann Marie looked through the peephole and saw a beautiful woman standing on the other side of the door. As soon as she turned the locks and opened the door, Mackie and his crew forced their way into the apartment followed by the woman. Mackie gave Ann Marie a backhand slap across her face, the force of which knocked her to the floor, as the other men quickly went through the rest of the apartment to make sure no one else was there. They signaled to Mackie that the apartment was clear.

"Hay gyal, you time come fi dead if you no do wah me want," said Mackie.

Ann Marie pleaded for her life. "Mackie, me never wan' do you nothing, Chuckie force me fi do it."

"Me know a force de boy force you fi do it." Mackie knew full well that he was going to kill her whether or not she complied with his wishes. "Listen, me no wan' do you nothing, a Chuckie me want, if you bring him yah fi me, me wi' gi' you a big money so you can lef' New

York."

Ann Marie was no fool. She knew she was in serious trouble. If Mackie didn't kill her, Chuckie's friends would certainly kill her for setting him up. She was in a no-win situation, but if she could buy time she may be able to figure a way out.

"Listen, me wan' you call Chuckie and tell him you haffi see him tonight."

"All me have fi him a him beeper number."

"Alright, me want you beep him, and when him call you back, no try no bullshit or me ago put a bullet right inna you head while you pon de phone, you hear me?"

"Me nah try nothing, me no deserve this, look from when me know you and Pam. Me nah dead fi Chuckie, me tell him no fi rob you."

This was the last place in the world Mackie wanted to be; he found no joy in doing what he knew he must now do. In his younger days, he would have killed her the first day they let him go and he would have gone after Chuckie and his entire family for robbing him. But now that he was older and had all the money he ever dreamed of, he no longer had the stomach for killing. Usually he left it up to others to do the dirty work for him. In fact, it took a lot of persuading from Mafia for Mackie to agree to make a move on Chuckie for Roy's killing. Mackie felt he was between a rock and a hard place, but he had no choice. He ran the risk of some of his men deserting him if he refused to avenge Roy's murder.

There was no mistake as to who killed Roy; Mafia was a witness to the shooting. Mafia had been leaving the Inn just as the first of two shots were fired. His reflexes had kicked in on time and he hit the ground and reached for his gun. He was able to peer through the door and see his partner laying on the pavement in a pool of blood. Then he saw a brown Volvo with two men in it as it sped away from the scene. Mafia was confident that Chuckie was the man he saw at the wheel of that car, and it was his belief that the other person in the vehicle must have been Stepper. The car was gone before he could get off a shot. Neither Chuckie nor Stepper saw Mafia, if they had it would have been a different story and Mafia knew it. Mafia didn't want them to see him and he definitely didn't want to confront them alone. Another five seconds and he would have been standing outside next to his friend and possibly laid out on the pavement dead right next to him. Mafia couldn't live with that thought; he had to get Chuckie and Stepper. Now he drew courage having Wakki and Obeyah next to him and he was confident that they could take Chuckie and Stepper down. Besides, he thought, Mackie was no slouch; he could hold his own.

Chuckie reached for his beeper and saw the code number 99. "A Ann Marie, cho, a wah she want now?" he said, to no one in particular. He checked his watch, it read 10:30 p.m. He picked up the receiver and dialed Ann Marie's number. "Ann Marie, wah happen?"

"No nothing, me no hear from you inna two days and me wan' see you."

"Right now is not a good time, me a go through some serious things right now."

"Chuckie, me haffi see you tonight, it important."

Mackie listened to her every word and his ear was pressed next to the receiver so he could hear Chuckie's response. He paid very close attention to the both of them.

Chuckie felt something was wrong, he was a master

of this type of game, both he and Stepper had perfected it. Now he would put her to the test, and depending on her answer he would know if it was a set up or not.

"Listen Ann Marie, me no deh too far from you, but me can't come right now, me ago send a youth come get you and bring you yah so."

Ann Marie got the message; she knew Chuckie was onto the game and that he knew she needed his help, but she had to take control of her emotions and respond in such a way so as not to alert Mackie. "No, me no wan' fi get dress and go no weh, me wan' you come check me fi a while, me need some buddy right now." Her comment about sex was meant to throw Mackie off, and it worked like a charm.

"Alright, me miss me pum-pum but me can't get deh till de next hour and a half, me haffi finish up some business first, then me can stay deh fi de rest a de night."

"Alright, me a wait pon you, come as soon as you can."

"Me wi' see you soon," said Chuckie as he hung up the phone. He turned to Dreaddy and Cow, Stepper was still in the bathroom washing his jacket. "Ann Marie inna trouble, somebody deh a de house a try lure me deh."

"A must de boy Mafia, that mean him have Mackie's blessings. De one Mackie could a deh deh too. So, wah you wan' we do?" asked Dreaddy.

Chuckie called Stepper out of the bathroom and explained what he thought was going on with Ann Marie. Stepper was pissed and ready to move out. Cow also made it clear that he wanted to make the move with the men. He felt this was his golden opportunity to prove himself to his friends, and also just to do something on behalf of Pops.

Chuckie was emotionally out of it thinking of Ann Marie. "A wan' tell unnu eno, you see dah little thing deh Ann Marie, I man check fi her eno, she do a good job fi mek me know seh it no safe a de house. The way she talk to me pon the phone she a make me know say somebody have her, me and her no talk about sex over de phone, come to think 'bout it, not even when me deh wid her we no talk like dat. The boy did a listen in pon de phone. Me a wonder if a really de boy Mackie. She set him up already and him know say she tight with me, me can't just lef her deh, she is a thing weh always deh deh fi me, I can't sit back and mek dem boy deh do her nothing. I man a go on deh and lick down everything inna de house."

"I man feel the same way, dem boy deh fi respect I and I," said Stepper.

"Mek we flash!" said Dreaddy.

"Yo, I a come wid unnu," demanded Cow.

"Cow, stay out a this," said Chuckie.

"To raas, me a stay out a it, me a do it fi Pops."

"Alright, get you forty-five," said Chuckie.

The Captain's office was filled with officers and several agents from the F.B.I. They were going over the paperwork they had just received. Albert Roberts was wanted in connection with the execution slaying of three individuals in Delaware.

"Okay gentlemen, we have a mass murderer on our hands. We have him tied to three killings in Delaware plus the five here in Brooklyn; that makes eight murders. We have to get him off the streets, dead or alive.

Peter Riley, one of the F.B.I. agents spoke up. "Captain McKenny, you have the full cooperation of the

101

Federal Government. We have agents on surveillance at the home of Chuckie's mother and we also have a team staking out the home of Stepper's parents. As soon as either one of them shows up or calls we'll have them."

"Okay," said the Captain, "Lieutenant I want that girl, Carol Wilson picked up and brought back to the station. We'll charge her with withholding information until she tells us where we can find these guys. I have a feeling she knows where in the city we can find both of them."

"Captain, I think we stand a better chance of getting these guys by leaving her on the streets. We already have a close eye on her; she can't make a move without our knowing."

"Okay, just make sure we don't lose her."

"I'll stay on top of it personally."

Captian McKenny's phone rang. "Captain McKenny here."

"Captain, this is Captain Connors from the Special Crime Task Force."

"Yes Captain Connors, what can I do for you?"

"There were two separate shootings in the Bronx. I have five bodies here that you may be interested in. Four of the victims were killed in or around a store which we believe was a marijuana outlet. It seems to have been a robbery gone bad. Two were bound in the store at the time of death, while the other two were found outside of the store. One of the victims outside the store was chased and gunned down on the street. The victims were all Jamaican. We have a witness who saw two men speed away in a gold colored Volvo Sedan. The other homicide occurred about an hour earlier. One Jamaican male was killed in that shooting; it was a straight up hit. Nothing was taken from the victim who was a Rastafarian. A Volvo was also seen at the scene of that shooting. We believe the five homicides are related."

"I'd like a full report on those homicides, and I want a ballistics report on the weapon or weapons used in those shootings as well," said Captian McKenny.

"I thought you would. From the preliminary investigation, a thirty-eight was used in the homicides at the store, but we're unable to ascertain what type of weapon was used in the other homicide. We're in the process of running ballistics on the bullets taken from both shootings. We'll compare it to the markings we have on your officer's missing weapon. I should have the results within the hour."

"I'll dispatch my lieutenant to your precinct right away, along with a few photos of our suspects and a warrant we received for one of them related to a triple homicide in Delaware."

"I'll be expecting him."

Captian McKenny hung up the phone and turned toward the men in the room. "Gentlemen, our suspect may be tied to five murders that occurred in the Bronx earlier today which brings his total to thirteen homicides. Get that son-of-a-bitch off my streets!"

Lieutenant Fisher and Sergeant Fuller were dispatched to Manhattan. When they entered the precinct they were directed to the Captain's office.

"Captain Connors, I'm Lieutenant Fisher and this is Sergeant Fuller."

"I've been expecting you; have a seat please. Gentlemen, we have a positive match. Your officer's weapon was used in both homicides here in the Bronx.

The first homicide was committed on Webster Avenue. The victim, male, was shot once in the head and we have a witness to the shooting, the victim's pregnant girlfriend. She was standing next to him when he was shot, and she said she can positively identify the shooter. She said he tried to shoot her as well but the gun didn't fire, so he turned and walked away and got into a Volvo. She thinks it was either brown or Gold."

"A brown Volvo?" asked Sergeant Fuller.

"Yes, brown or gold. Why?"

"One of our suspects owns a brown Volvo, a 1986 Turbo."

"Do you have a plate number?"

"Yes, we've already put out an all-points bulletin on it."

"New York plates?"

"Yes, registered in New York."

"Okay, he has to be our guy. In the second shooting, two guys were seen leaving the scene of the crime in a gold Volvo with New York plates, but the witness wasn't completely positive about the color."

"Captain, I've brought a few photos of our two suspects, and I also have a warrant for Albert Roberts, a.k.a. Stepper. I'd like to have the witness take a look at the photos," said Lieutenant Fisher.

"Our witness was admitted into Lincoln Hospital. We can take a ride, show her the pictures and see if she recognizes any of these guys."

At the hospital a police guard was posted outside the room. The officers entered the room and showed the pictures to the witness. She picked out Stepper as the man who shot her boyfriend. But she was unable to identify the man driving the getaway car.

After leaving the room Lieutenant Fisher used the pay phone to call his Captain.

"Captain, Fisher here."

"Yes Lieutenant, are there any new developments?"

"We have a positive match on the weapon used in the homicides. It was Officer McCoy's gun that was in both shootings. We also have a witness to one of the homicides; she positively identified Stepper as the shooter. She couldn't identify Chuckie as being his accomplice, however, in both shootings Stepper was accompanied by someone. We have a make on a brown or gold Volvo with New York plates in both homicides."

"Good work. Our boy Chuckie drives a brown Volvo. I want you back here as soon as possible," said the Captain.

"I'm about to head over to the crime scenes; I'll head back to the office as soon as I complete my investigation."

"Very well. See you then."

Chapter 8

Mackie sat restless in the living room. The clock on the wall read 10:45 p.m. He could think of a million places he'd rather be than where he was. He kept trying to reassure himself that he had no choice. He had to be here, there was no other way.

Ann Marie was lying on her bed with her hands and feet tied. Mackie had a forty-four magnum revolver, Mafia carried a Tech-nine semi-automatic, Wakki carried a Mac-ten, and Obeyah had a pair of nine millimeters; they were armed to the teeth.

In Jamaica Wakki was known to have been responsible for the killing of at least 200 people on the island; it was a reputation that he relished. He felt he was untouchable and that no one could out gun him. Everything about him spelled death. He rarely smiled, kept very few friends, and he trusted no one. He had always been tight with Mackie, however, and had pulled the trigger for him on many occasions. Mackie brought him to America for that sole purpose and Wakki had no intention of letting his friend down. Wakki stood five feet, ten inches and weighed a hundred and eighty pounds. His complexion was very dark, he kept his hair cut low and very neat, and he maintained a clean shaved face.

Obeyah was a very attractive woman. She stood five feet, seven inches, weighed a hundred and forty-five pounds and had a body to die for. Her complexion was a shade lighter than Wakki's, her hair was long and black, well kept and neat. She wore nothing but the finest clothes that money could buy – the very definition of a high maintenance woman. She had always used her looks to get by in life, and when she hooked up with Wakki and Mackie she turned to setting up men and carrying out hits for Mackie. She was credited for at least 50 bodies in Jamaica.

Mafia stood six feet, two inches and weighed a solid two hundred and ten pounds. He was brown skinned with low cut hair and clean shaven. He had always been Mackie's ace, their friendship originating back to their school days in Jamaica. Mackie held him in high regard and would do just about anything for him, so bringing him to America and making him a lieutenant in his organization was an easy choice. From the day Mafia arrived in America he never needed anything.

Mackie stood five feet ten inches, and weighed two hundred and thirty pounds. He had a large stomach, dark complexion, a neatly cut beard, and he kept his hair cut low. He had a rough life as a child and had to fight viciously for everything he got, but as he reached the top of his game, and age started setting in, he longed more for peace than for war. However, he found it more and more difficult to achieve that goal. Someone was always eagerly awaiting to take what he had worked, stolen or killed for over the years. Like his friends, he had many bodies under his belt, so many that he had lost count a long time ago. Although all four of these individuals had been involved in crime all their lives, Mackie was able to elevate himself above the rest; he was the boss and the money maker. He no longer had the stomach for violence, but he knew in his line of work that it was as unavoidable as death is to the living.

Chuckie parked around the block from Ann Marie's apartment building and the men checked their weapons.

"Alright, listen, we can't just walk up deh and ring de bell, me bet me life de boy dem a watch de front a de building from de front window. Wah me wan' we do a this. Stepper, me wan' you, Dreaddy and Cow fi go up pon de roof a de building next door and cross over to her building and take de fire escape down to her third floor apartment. Stepper done know her window. Just wait deh till you hear me kick it off from de front door. Me know once de pussy dem see me come inna de building them a go try fi take me right a Ann Marie's apartment door," said Chuckie.

"Me no too like de idea a you a go inna de building alone," said Stepper.

"Me want dem fi think say me come alone, so dem wi' focus pon de front door, then unnu can force de window open and ease inna de apartment pon dem."

"Alright, mek we mek it happen, fly de trunk mek me get de crowbar fi open de window," said Dreaddy.

Chuckie popped the trunk and Dreaddy retrieved the crowbar. Chuckie wore a vest and carried a nine millimeter along with the thirty-eight police special. Stepper wore a vest and carried a nine millimeter and a Mac-ten. Dreaddy wore a vest and carried a nine millimeter and the Mac-ten that he brought back from the

Bronx. Cow was the only one without a vest, and he carried the forty-five automatic that the men had recently given him.

"Stepper, mek sure unnu take care a Cow," said Chuckie.

"You know me nah mek nothing happen to him, him have we money and him still have a works fi we." Stepper grinned.

Chuckie smiled back as they went their separate ways. Stepper led the way as Dreaddy and Cow followed close behind. Chuckie made his way slowly to Ann Marie's building. He kept his hand in his pocket with his fingers wrapped tightly around his nine millimeter, ready for anything. Ann Marie was heavy on his mind. He hoped he was all wrong about this and that all was well with her. What if he was being paranoid and had made too much of his conversation with her on the phone? Even if so, better to be safe than sorry. He shook off this train of thought as he approached the entrance to the building, and readied himself for the unexpected.

Stepper, Dreaddy and Cow entered the adjacent apartment building. The buildings were connected with no separation from one roof to the other which made access much easier. There was only a very low dividing structure, more for decoration than to keep anyone out, and easy to simply step over. There were six of these connected buildings on this side of the block.

The men made their way down Ann Marie's fire escape as Chuckie entered her building. Just as Chuckie had predicted, he was being watched from the window.

Mafia peeped through the curtain and looked out the window, observing Chuckie entering the building; he was sure there was no way Chuckie could have seen him.

"Mackie! De pussy a come."

"Alright gyal, me no wan' you mek no noise, as me tell you before, me nah go hurt you, a him me want. This no have nothing fi do wid you," said Mackie.

Ann Marie nodded, too afraid to speak. She saw her entire life passing before her, and a million thoughts raced through her mind, especially how she wished she had never meet Chuckie. She knew Mackie would kill her, there was no way he was going to leave a witness behind to finger him someday.

Wakki busied himself stuffing a rag into Ann Marie's mouth.

"Obeyah, when him ring de bell open de door and tell him you a Ann Marie's friend, him no know you so him nah go think no way, we ago inna de bathroom, just mek him walk pass de bathroom then we wi' hold him," said Mackie.

Stepper, Dreaddy and Cow crouched down next to Ann Marie's Window, but the blinds were drawn shut and they were unable to see what was happening in the apartment. Dreaddy held the crowbar at the ready and they all listened keenly, waiting for the signal to move.

Chuckie's adrenaline was at its peak. He tried to think of every possible approach they may come at him with and concluded that he would take deadly action if anything at all seemed out of the norm. He continued gripping his gun with his right hand and he cocked it, keeping his hand in his pocket as he approached the door cautiously. He rang the bell using his left hand. Within a few seconds the door swung open and there before him stood one of the most attractive women he had ever seen. He tried his best to place her face but could not; he was sure he'd never seen her before and something wasn't right about her. Every fiber in his body told him he was in danger. He quickly reflected on his chain but there was nothing; he wasn't experiencing the pain in his neck that he had in Harlem earlier when he was in danger. Even so, something just didn't feel right about being in the presence of this beautiful woman; maybe the chain was warning him in a different way. Chuckie kept his eyes on the woman, taking in everything about her. He noted that she was dressed in a pantsuit with an oversized jacket and her beauty was alluring. He quickly erased that thought from his mind and refocused on the business at hand.

"Hi Chuckie, I'm Jennifer, Ann Marie's friend from Connecticut. She ask me fi get de door fi you, she's expecting you. I was just getting ready to leave, I have a long drive back home. Ann Marie is waiting for you in the bedroom."

Chuckie definitely smelled a rat now. If this woman was leaving why the hell didn't Ann Marie walk her to the door? He decided to make his move. He got close to her as if he was going to walk past her, then with lightning speed he grabbed her around her neck with his left hand and rested his nine millimeter on her temple.

"Don't say another word." As he held her tightly against his body he felt the unmistakable bulge of a gun rubbing against him. He was definitely in danger and this woman was sent to lure him in. He wanted to kill her right then and there, but didn't want to alert whoever was awaiting him in the apartment. Chuckie knew the layout of the place like the back of his hand. The nearest room to the front door was the bathroom and he figured that would be the logical place for someone to ambush him.

Obeyah was no fool, and she wasn't frightened at all. She knew she had to do something to alert the rest of the men in the apartment, but she knew that if she tried to break free while his gun was still on her temple she'd be dead. She had to do something in a hurry, but what? She decided to raise her voice. "Chuckie wah you a do?" she hollered.

Chuckie wasn't slow, he knew exactly what she was doing, but for some reason he didn't want to take her life so easily. He released his grip on her and violently pushed her away from him, knowing full well that she was armed. He kept his eyes trained on her as he held his gun to his side. He had a strange need to see what she was made of, to test her ability.

Obeyah flipped over and came up with two nine millimeters in her hands.

Chuckie was surprised by her speed, but he was faster. He never took his eyes off of her, and since he already had the drop on her, he squeezed the trigger twice. Both bullets tore through her left breast and she died instantly. The gunshots alerted Mackie and Wakki who rushed out of the bathroom with guns drawn. Obeyah lay dead in front of the bathroom door and Mackie and Wakki hesitated for a split second when they saw her. That was all the time Chuckie needed and he opened fire on the pair, hitting Mackie twice in the stomach and grazing Wakki's left shoulder. Wakki recovered quickly and let loose a barrage of shots from his Mac-ten. Chuckie hit the floor hard, taking a slug square in his chest. The vest saved his life, stopping the slug from entering his body, but the wind was knocked out of him and his chest felt as though someone had hit him with a sledge hammer. The pain rushed straight to his head and he felt lightheaded, but he knew he'd be dead if he passed out, and his drive to survive was stronger than the immediate pain and dizziness he was experiencing. He kept his eyes open and his gun trained in the direction of Wakki.

When the first set of gunshots sounded, Dreaddy slid the crowbar into the base of the window and pried it open, allowing the three of them to access the bedroom where Ann Marie was tied up. Dreaddy quickly entered the room followed by Stepper and Cow. Mafia had just left the bedroom to investigate what was taking place in the front of the apartment which gave Dreaddy, Stepper and Cow the necessary time to enter unnoticed.

Stepper signaled Cow to untie Ann Marie as he and Dreaddy slowly made their way to the front of the apartment, each carrying a Mac-ten. As the second volley of shots sounded, Dreaddy eased up on Mafia from behind and, resting the nuzzle of his Mac-ten at the back of Mafia's head, he slowly squeezed the trigger. Two quick bursts from the Mac-ten tore through Mafia's head. His forehead exploded and he fell limp, dead before he hit the floor; blood was everywhere.

Chuckie was sprawled on the floor feeling like his chest was on fire; the pain was intense. But even with the pain, he felt a sense of ease knowing the vest had stopped the bullet. Suddenly he heard shots coming from the back of the apartment and he knew his partners were making their move. He fired a few shots in the direction of Wakki to keep him busy, but Wakki answered with his own volley of shots.

Wakki was concerned about the two shots he heard coming from the back of the apartment, but he quickly concluded that it was probably Mafia shooting Ann

Marie, so he kept his focus on Chuckie. He glanced down at his boss, Mackie, on the floor bleeding badly. He would need to get medical help in a hurry or he wouldn't survive. The thought of his boss dying suddenly made him nuts and he got wicked, turning up the heat on Chuckie, trying to get it over with in a hurry. But at that very instant, Stepper eased up on him, taking careful aim, and squeezed the trigger of his Mac-ten. The burst was deafening with ten shots hitting Wakki, killing him instantly and tearing his body to pieces.

Stepper signaled to Chuckie that all was well. Chuckie stood up and walked over to Mackie, who was still alive, holding his stomach, groaning and bleeding to death. Chuckie's nine millimeter was empty so he reached into his waistband and retrieved the thirty-eight police special. Without saying a word, he pointed it at the side of Mackie's head and squeezed the trigger twice. Mackie's body went limp.

"Chuckie!" said Stepper, "We haffi lef yah so."

Chuckie went into the bedroom, hugged Ann Marie, placed a blanket around her shoulders and led her out of the apartment.

Pandemonium broke loose in the 71st Precinct when the call came in that there was a quadruple homicide at 2172 Eastern Parkway. Lieutenant Fisher and Sergeant Fuller responded to the call. When they arrived at the scene an army of police cruisers and other emergency vehicles were already parked in front of the building.

The Lieutenant approached a uniformed officer. "What's the current situation Sergeant?"

"We have four bodies on the third floor in apartment 3-C. Homicide should be here shortly."

"Okay, make sure the crime scene is sealed off and no one enters that apartment until the detectives arrive."

"It's being sealed off as we speak, sir."

Detective Majors and Det. Williams pulled up as the uniformed sergeant walked back into the building. Shortly after that, Detectives Buchanan and Bradley from the Special Crime Task Force also arrived on the scene.

Inside the apartment the group of detectives from different agencies came up on three bodies laying in the hallway. One female and two males. And on further investigation, a fourth body was found in the living room.

The lieutenant took a close look at the female then walked over to the two males. "Damn! That's Mackie; our boys must be tied into this. There must be a connection here with Roy's murder earlier today. I knew we'd be hearing from Mr. Mackie before the day was done. Gentlemen, we have a serious situation here. I want to know whose apartment this is and I want the identification on the rest of these victims." He made his way into the living room next to take a closer look at the fourth body. He couldn't identify the guy.

The uniformed sergeant entered the apartment accompanied by the building superintendent. The superintendent looked at the female victim and told the officers that she was not the woman who lived there. The Lieutenant asked for the name of the woman who rented the apartment.

"The apartment is rented to Ann Marie Johnson."

"Does she live here alone?"

"Yes, but I've seen her with a tall guy from time to time. I assume it's her boyfriend. I don't think he lives here though, he just visits her."

"Detective Majors, have him take a look at our

suspects to see if he can identify any of them."

Detective Majors went to his vehicle and returned with a file containing the pictures of Chuckie and Stepper. The superintendent identified Chuckie as the guy he'd often seen coming and going from the apartment.

"Bingo," said the Lieutenant. "Everything is falling into place. Will you come down to the station and give a formal statement?"

"Absolutely, I'll cooperate in any way possible."

"Gentlemen," said the Lieutenant, "I want a full report as soon as everything is wrapped up here." With that, Lieutenant Fisher and Sergeant Fuller left the apartment, along with the building superintendent, and headed for the precinct.

Chapter 9

Chuckie brought the vehicle to a full stop in front of Cow's apartment building. Cow, Stepper, Dreaddy and Ann Marie climbed from the vehicle and went into the building.

Chuckie kept his eyes on Ann Marie until she made it through the front door and he could no longer see her. He felt a deep sense of sorrow for what she had been through, knowing that he was the cause of it. He would have to make it up to her somehow. He shifted his vehicle into first gear and pulled off to find a parking space around the corner. After parking the vehicle, he came back to the building and climbed the stairs to Cow's apartment. Cow stood at the apartment door waiting for him. Chuckie joined the rest of the men in the apartment; they needed to plan their next move.

Ann Marie was clearly shaken. She hadn't said a word since leaving her apartment, and the expression on her face was that of a woman who was terrified, one who had retreated deep inside herself. Chuckie was worried about her and his attempts to bring her around were useless; she wasn't responsive. She was probably in need of some kind of medical attention, but that was clearly out of the question for the time being. The other men were worried about her as well.

Stepper was extremely worried about her in a different sense than the others, she had been a witness to a quadruple homicide. Stepper hadn't been fond of Ann Marie from the first day he met her. As far as he was concerned, she was too money hungry and that in itself was enough to make him wary of her. If it had been up to him he would have left her to her fate with Mackie. But on the other hand, knowing how Chuckie felt about her, it would have been extremely difficult on him if she had died at the hands of Mackie. Deep down Stepper knew they made the right decision in saving her, and if he had it to do all over again he wouldn't change a thing. But he couldn't help wondering about whether or not she could be trusted, based on the way she was reacting right now.

Cow made a strong drink for Ann Marie, which she gulped down as if there was no tomorrow. Slowly she began to relax as the alcohol began to kick in.

Chuckie was still in pain from the bullet striking him in the chest, and again he thanked his lucky stars for the vest he wore. "Cow, you have any pain killer?"

"Me have some inna de medicine cabinet."

As Chuckie walked in the direction of the bathroom, Stepper quickly cut off his path to speak to him. They both entered the bathroom where they could talk out of earshot of Ann Marie and the rest of the men. Chuckie opened the medicine cabinet, found the pain killers and took four of them. Then he removed his vest to inspect himself. He had a nasty bruise on his chest and there was a hole in the outer layer of the vest. He poked his finger in the hole and felt the bullet resting in the bottom lining. "Damn de vest dem yah real good, a de best investment we ever mek."

"So how de I feel?" asked Stepper.

"Me cool still, me just a feel little pain."

"Yo, Chuckie! Me no know 'bout dah gyal deh."

"Wah you a talk 'bout?"

"Chuckie , me just have a bad feeling 'bout her. She know too much and me no think we can run de risk in trusting her given de way she a gwaan."

"She wouldn't do anything fi hurt we."

"I hope you nah make you personal feelings cloud you judgment. Wah we ago do wid her anyway?"

"She cool man, we can take her go a Bronx and mek she chill out wid Pops' baby mother fi awhile, then we can mek arrangements fi send her go a Florida go chill with her people dem."

"Me brother, as much as me no like fi say this, me think de I a mek a mistake, de babylon dem a go trace de apartment to her, and wid four bodies in deh, dem a go raise hell fi find her, de only safe way out a this we haffi brush her. That a de only way dem can't tie we to de body dem. Plus, you see how she look out deh?"

"I man know wah you a say, but me know she's a trooper, and how it a go look fi we go through all a that shit fi save her life fi turn around and tek it. She nah go turn 'gainst we."

"Alright! Me a go gi' you dah one yah, but the first sign me get say she a go flip or she can't take de pressure, me ago brush her."

"You no haffi worry 'bout dat, if me feel seh she a slip me wi' brush her meself. Just leave her to me, me wi' deal wid her," said Chuckie.

By the time Stepper and Chuckie came back to the living room, Ann Marie was back to her old self and talking. She was in the process of thanking Cow and Dreaddy when Chuckie and Stepper entered the room. Chuckie felt good to see she was back to her old self. He glanced over at Stepper to acknowledge that she was alright, but Stepper didn't seem to share that sentiment as he turned his focus away from Chuckie and intently onto Ann Marie.

When Chuckie reentered the room, Ann Marie practically raced over to him and hugged and kissed him passionately. She began to cry and assured him that if it hadn't been for him she would be dead. Chuckie hugged her tightly; he had sincere feelings for her.

Stepper watched them closely, still feeling that it was a major mistake to leave her alive. Then it hit him like a bomb; his best friend was in love with this woman.

Chuckie sat Ann Marie down and explained to her that he wanted her to stay in the Bronx for a while until he could make arrangements for her to go to Florida. She accepted the offer but was concerned about her property. He told her she would have to leave it all behind and start over. This didn't sit well with her, as she had a lot of money and jewelry hidden in the apartment. She kept it to herself however, and didn't mention it to Chuckie. She figured that somehow she would be able to retrieve them without his knowledge. She had no intention of going to Florida without her things.

By now it was midnight and the body count was at fourteen. Cow went to his bedroom and retrieved the $15,000 he'd made from the sale of the crack cocaine. The men split it up equally.

They felt it best that Chuckie make the trip to the Bronx alone, accompanied by Ann Marie. Chuckie left his car with Stepper and borrowed Cow's Maxima for the trip since the Volvo may have been seen at one of the earlier shootings. Chuckie and Ann Marie headed out of Brooklyn.

Stepper and Dreaddy chilled out with Cow, smoking a few spliffs.

"Cow," said Stepper, "Me wan' go pick up I ride and check you back tomorrow."

"Alright, me wi' drop you off a you ride."

"Listen," said Dreaddy, "I a go a my yard, so right now me wi' tek de Volvo and drop off Stepper and come check unnu back in a de morning."

"Alright, dat cool cause I kinda tired right now, a nuff work I put in tonight," said Cow. The men laughed knowing that Cow never fired a shot, but as far as Stepper and Dreaddy were concerned, he had handled himself well.

Stepper looked over at Cow. "Me bredda, you do real good tonight, me wi' go anyway wid you and feel safe knowing seh you nah back down and lef you friend dem."

Dreaddy agreed.

Cow was all smiles. He felt he had finally arrived and was now a full member of the crew. He felt a true sense of love and acceptance from these men. He knew he would be willing to die for them and was confident they would do the same for him. Cow walked Stepper and Dreaddy to the door.

Stepper and Dreaddy walked to where the Volvo was parked around the corner. As they pulled away from the curb, Stepper said to Dreaddy, "Me bredda, me worried about leaving de gyal alive, me think is a big mistake."

"Cho, Chuckie know wah him a do, you know if him

couldn't trust her him would a lick her down."

"Me know wah you a say, but Chuckie deeply in love wid her right now, and me just feel seh him a mek him heart do de thinking fi him."

"Cho, you know Chuckie better than dat, even if him love her him nah go mek she bring we down, mek we gi' him a chance wid her."

"I hope you right. Anyway, de I fi careful wid de Volvo, it might a hot by now. Mek sure you park it round de block from you house, and careful how you approach it in a de morning."

"Yea mon, me done think 'bout dat. So wah you a go do fi de rest a de night?"

"I a go flash go check me gyal Carol round a de 90s," replied Stepper.

"De man fi careful round deh, you know dem boy deh a fight 'gainst we fi a long time now," said Dreaddy.

"Dem boy deh no wan' no serious beef wid we."

Dreaddy pulled up next to Stepper's BMW and Stepper got out and into his own car. Stepper rolled down the window and looked his friend straight in the eye. They had so much respect and love for each other.

"Weh you no leave de Volvo yah so and mek me gi' you a ride home?"

Dreaddy ruled against it. "Listen, me a go park de car inna me mother garage, me wan' take it off a de street. Plus me no think it wise fi lef it yah so, it too close to Chuckie's house."

"Alright, tomorrow!" Stepper pulled away from the curb.

As Dreaddy drove to Atlantic Avenue heading toward Bushwick he noticed a police cruiser behind him driven by two white police officers. It would be just his luck to get pulled over by some white cops who couldn't wait to pull over a black man in an expensive car. He told himself to keep cool. Nothing had happened yet; maybe they were just fishing - hoping he'd give them a reason to pull him over. He was careful to stay below the speed limit. He was armed with his nine millimeter and the Mac-ten. He decided to make a few detours to see if they would follow him. He turned onto Jefferson Avenue and the cruiser also made the turn. He was sure now that he was being followed. He felt the butterflies in his stomach, and at that moment he knew he'd have to have a showdown with these officers because there was no way they were going to take him in alive. He ever so gently eased his nine millimeter out of his waistband and placed it under his right thigh. If the officers had him in their sights, he didn't want to make any sudden moves that would alert them to the danger they faced. The only way out for him would be to get the upper hand; it could very well mean the difference between his living or dying. Dreaddy reassured himself, if those officers stopped him and approached his vehicle he would open fire on them without any hesitation.

The police officers trailing Dreaddy had called in the plates and the make of the vehicle and the call came back that the vehicle was implicated in a multiple homicide. The officers were told not to approach, but to keep the vehicle in sight at all times; other units were en route to intercept.

Lieutenant Fisher was wrapping up the superintendent's statement when the call came in that Chuckie's Volvo was spotted. His heart raced, this was the break he'd been waiting for. He ran from his office and met up with Sergeant Fuller and the two detectives from the Special Crime Task Force. "Men this is it," he yelled as the four men quickly made their way to their vehicles. The Lieutenant got on the radio and spoke directly to the two officers who were trailing the Volvo. "Car Fifty-one, this is Lieutenant Fisher from the 71st Precinct."

"Car Fifty-one here, Lieutenant."

"Fifty-one, what is your location?"

"We're east on Jefferson heading towards Dunly."

"How many occupants are in the vehicle?"

"From the looks of it there's only the driver," replied the Officer.

"Okay Fifty-one, do not approach the vehicle under any circumstances, the suspect is armed and extremely dangerous. Keep a close eye on the vehicle, we are en route."

"Will do, sir."

Dreaddy wondered why they were following him but not pulling him over; something didn't sit right with him. *Oh fuck it!* Why should he care if they noticed him reaching for something in the car or not. He quickly reached over and pulled his duffel bag next to him, unzipped it and pulled out the Mac-ten. He put a round into the chamber and then stuck his nine millimeter back into his waistband. He pulled over next to a store and left the engine running.

The sudden move caught the officers off guard and a slight panic set in as they thought about what to do next. The officer behind the wheel was determined not to let Dreaddy get away. This capture could bring him a gold star - his first, and could definitely advance his career in the force. He said to his partner, "We have to approach him before he exits the car."

"We have to call it in," replied the second officer.

"There's no fucking time for that shit, we have to move now! We can take the son-of-a-bitch, it's only one nigga!" said the lead officer as he hit the switch for the emergency lights and brought the cruiser to a halt directly behind the Volvo. He stepped out of the cruiser, not waiting for his partner, and quickly approached the Volvo with his gun drawn. His partner was on the radio giving their location when he heard the deafening burst of the Mac-ten. From the car he watched horrified, as his partner got hit in the upper body and face; he was dead before he hit the ground. The second officer panicked as he shouted over his radio, "Officer down! Officer Down!" He jumped out of his cruiser and emptied his nine millimeter in Dreaddy's direction. Several shots tore through the rear windshield, shattering it completely.

Dreaddy was not hit and he returned fire from the Mac-ten as squad cars began arriving from every direction. The situation quickly turned into a running gun battle as Dreaddy safely exited the Volvo and made his way on foot, trying to evade the officers pursuing him. The neighborhood became a scene from a wild west shootout, bullets flying everywhere.

Lieutenant Fisher and Sergeant Fuller pulled up and joined the shootout, aiming their weapons in the direction of Dreaddy, where he was hunkered down between two parked cars.

Dreaddy opened up the Mac-ten with a full burst, hitting and instantly killing a uniformed officer.

Detective Buchanan seized the opportunity, took

careful aim, then squeezed his trigger. The bullet hit Dreaddy square in the chest knocking him backward against one of the parked cars.

The vest prevented the bullet from penetrating his body, but the wind was knocked out of him. Dreaddy quickly recovered, regained his focus, and sprayed the Mac-ten in the direction of Detective Buchanan.

The detective realized the obvious, and while staying low, called out to the other officers. "He's wearing a vest!"

Dreaddy opened up another barrage of shots as he ran toward an apartment building and into the lobby. His chest felt like it was on fire but he didn't have time to think about it, he had to survive. He took cover on the first flight of steps and trained his weapon on the entrance of the apartment building.

Sergeant Fuller rushed in with his gun drawn and Dreaddy let loose a full blast from the Mac-ten. Sergeant Fuller was hit several times with one bullet striking him in the center of his forehead. He fell dead, his blood slowly spreading across the lobby floor.

Lieutenant Fisher and several others rushed into the lobby. Seeing the body of his partner filled him with sorrow and rage. Fisher knelt down next to his partner with tears in his eyes and checked for vital signs; there were none. Fisher looked up at the officers standing over him. "Get that son-of-a-bitch, don't let him get away!"

They all raced out with the Lieutenant bringing up the rear.

Dreaddy had made his way to the roof of the building with Lieutenant Fisher and the rest of the officers in hot pursuit. Just as he got to the fire escape and was about to make his descent, he turned in the direction of the roof's door and found himself looking into the barrels of several weapons all pointed directly at him. He attempted to raise the Mac-ten into a firing posture but wasn't quick enough; the officers opened fire on him, hitting him multiple times all over his upper torso. One shot from a three fifty-seven magnum caught him square in the face, the exit tearing away the entire back of his head. The force of the impact propelled him over the ledge of the four story building and he was dead before he hit the pavement.

Stepper drove past Carol's house being as vigilant as ever about his surroundings. He quickly spotted two white guys sitting in a car not far from Carol's house and right away he suspected they were police. He continued slowly past them without glancing over, and once he turned the corner he parked and made his way back to carol's house on foot. He detoured through a few backyards, then made his way to the back of her house and rang the bell from the back entrance. Soon Carol came to the door. She quickly opened it and let him in, then they made their way back to her upstairs apartment.

"Stepper, police all over de place a look fi you, me neva have no number fi get in touch wid you fi warn you, but you haffi careful dem a watch de house."

"Yea, me see dem out deh. Wah dem say dem wan' me fa?"

"Dem say dem want talk to you 'bout a murder, and dem want question you 'bout a police weh get rob down de street from me Sunday night."

"Wah you tell dem?"

"Me tell dem me no see you in over a week, and me

no know weh you live."

"How dem know fi come check you?" asked Stepper.

"Me hear say dem did round a 91st street a rough up Sammy dem, a must dem send dem come yah."

"That mek sense, dah boy deh Sammy a fight 'gainst I a long time now, but me would a neva think him would a turn to police fi get I. Well me guess him figure it better de police dem deal wid me than fi him deal wid I. Alright, if a so de wicked boy wan' play, me wi' deal wid him case."

From that moment on Stepper vowed to get Sammy, no more putting him off. He was set on paying Sammy a visit before the police and he encountered each other. Stepper had no love for the police and there was no way they would take him alive. In his mind, anyone cooperating with them was his enemy and an open target for him.

Carol didn't mention that she had been taken to the police station and questioned; there was no way she was going to tell him she picked out Chuckie's mug shot for the police. He would kill her if he ever found out.

Stepper was one step ahead of her. He didn't trust her all that much and he felt she knew more than she was letting on, but he didn't want to put her on defense by pressing the issue. Sooner or later she would slip up and reveal her hand. He hoped he wouldn't have to hurt this woman because deep down he truly had feelings for her. But if it came down to it, he wouldn't hesitate to take her life if he discovered she was providing information to the police.

Stepper decided to pick her brain and lay a trap for her to fall into at a later date if she was lying. "So weh you did deh earlier when me did a call you?"

"Me deh yah all day except fi when me go down a me mother yard. Wah time you did a call me?"

"Me no too sure a de time, some time inna de evening."

"A must a when me did deh a me mother," said Carol.

"Listen," said Stepper, "Me wan' chill out wid you tonight, but me no wan' we stay yah so. Put on some clothes and mek we get a hotel room."

Carol was reluctant; deep down she feared this man, but at the same time she was turned on by him and the fear he instilled in her. Her gut was telling her not to leave with him, but she had never been the type of woman to exercise good judgment or listen to her intuition. If she were, she would not have started a relationship with Stepper in the first place. She knew she had to leave with him; she really didn't have any choice. If she refused to go with him it would only raise red flags in his mind, and the last thing she needed was for him to become suspicious of her. Reluctantly she agreed to go.

They made their way to the back of the house, keeping out of sight of the two police officers stationed across the street from Carol's house. Carol followed closely behind Stepper and they made it to the car without being noticed. Stepper started the car then unlocked the door for Carol. She got in and sat next to him as he drove off and out of the neighborhood.

They made it away safely and Stepper breathed a sigh of relief. The couple checked into a hotel off of Fulton Street as husband and wife. The hotel room was clean and neat, a suite with one bedroom and bath. Stepper could now relax and get some badly needed rest. It had been one hell of a day. He reassured himself that he was safe now that he was far away from Carol's house where the police surveillance was going on. And yet something nagged at him; he still had a strange feeling that Carol wasn't being completely truthful with him concerning the police but he decided to let it go for now.

Stepper stretched out on the bed with Carol in his arms. The television set was turned on but he wasn't paying much attention to it until a sudden news flash came on channel eleven. A young reporter appeared on the screen. "Three police officers and a suspect were killed in a blazing gun battle in Bushwick."

Stepper was now very focused; the television had his full attention as he listened closely to the report. The camera zoomed in for a close-up shot of the crime scene, and that's when Stepper caught sight of the Volvo. The rear window was shot out, but he was confident it was Chuckie's car. He kept his cool, not wanting to alert Carol.

"Mon, what this world coming to, everyday people a dead before dem time, even de police no safe," said Carol.

Stepper said nothing as a million things swirled through his mind. He needed to give Chuckie a call and get out of Brooklyn in a hurry. "Carol, me a tek a walk go a de corner store, you want anything fi eat?"

"Me alright, just get me something fi drink."

Stepper got up from the bed, tucked his nine millimeter in his waistband, donned his army jacket and headed out the door.

Chuckie was airing out the Maxima, reaching speeds of seventy to eighty miles per hour. The Franklin Delanore Roosevelt Parkway was clear of traffic and the

night breeze was cool under the light of the full moon.
Ann Marie sat next to him, relaxing and enjoying the
music of Yellow Man. As she tapped her finger to the
steady rhythm of the words, "I'm getting married in the
morning", Chuckie's beeper buzzed.

He checked the code, it read 45. That was Stepper.
Stepper rarely beeped him, so it had to be important.
"Ann Marie, write down dah number yah fi me, get de
pen out a de glove compartment."

She retrieved the pen and wrote it down as Chuckie
relayed the number to her. Chuckie had just been heading
out of Harlem when the beeper sounded, but now he
looked for the nearest exit; he needed to find a phone
booth.

"Stepper, wah happen?" asked Chuckie.

"De police boy dem lick down Dreaddy."

"Wah, how dat happen?"

"I man just see it pon de news. Him just drop I off a I
ride and did a tek de Volvo go lock off a him mother
house. De boy dem pon de news say it was a shootout
between de police and an unidentified man. I see de car
pon de screen a so I know seh a him. I no know nothing
more but dem say three police boy get lick down."

"Yo, it no safe a Brooklyn right now, de I fi flash
come a Bronx. Weh Cow deh?"

"We lef him a him yard."

"Alright, shoot come a Bronx, I wi' see you when you
reach," said Chuckie.

"You wan' see, me have me gyal Carol wid me."

"Wah, you still go back go check dah gyal deh. De I
fi just lef' her deh, don't bring her wid you," said
Chuckie.

"You wan' see--"

"Hold on deh," Chuckie cut him off as he placed more coins in the phone. "Wah you did a say?" asked Chuckie.

"You wan' see, de police boy dem check Carol and ask fi I, and two boy a watch her house."

"How dem know say you involve wid her?"

"I no know fi sure but me check say de boy Sammy gi' I up," replied Stepper.

"Yo, me no trust dah gyal deh, a she could a call de police dem, de I fi just put a bullet inna her head and lef' her."

Stepper laughed.

"Wah you a laugh 'bout?"

"It kind a funny; me a tell you fi do the same thing earlier and you wouldn't do it."

"Yea, but things different now, is a whole new ball game," said Chuckie.

"Yo, Carol no have nothing pon we. Wah she can tell de babylon dem, say me did a grind her off? Right now I and I problem a de gyal weh you a ride wid. I wi' see you later." Stepper hung the phone up.

Chuckie knew his friend was right. He had to get rid of Ann Marie. Police killings were too big a deal to leave to chance.

When Chuckie returned to the car his demeanor had changed and Ann Marie sensed it. "Wah happen Chuckie?"

"No nothing, Stepper just want me fi check a youth fi him in a de Bronx." Chuckie pulled away from the corner and started driving, in what seemed to Ann Marie to be circles. Soon he pulled onto a dark street and before Ann Marie knew what was happening, Chuckie's nine millimeter was resting on her left breast. Without saying a word, he fired two shots, piercing her heart. He reached over her body, opened the door, and pushed her body out of the vehicle. He did his best not to look in her face as she rolled out, then he reached over the still warm passenger seat, slammed the door shut and sped off with tears in his eyes. He wished he could undo what he had just done; this was the hardest kill he had ever committed.

Chuckie drove to a twenty-four hour car wash where he scrubbed the car clean of any sign of Ann Marie's blood.

An hour later Chuckie pulled up in front of Pops' marijuana building, parked down the street and sat in the car reflecting on Ann Marie, only emptiness in his eyes. He kept telling himself that he had to do what he did; it couldn't be avoided. Then he thought of Dreaddy and that brought him out of his daze. He got out of the vehicle and went into the building.

Chapter 10

Captian McKenny strode through the front door of the apartment building and stopped in his tracks when he saw Lieutenant Fisher kneeling over Sergeant Fuller's body. Anger filled him as he took in the scene and saw the tears on Fisher's face.

The Captain approached him. "Lieutenant!"

The sound of the Captain's voice momentarily snapped Fisher out of his grief. "Yes Captain?"

"Let's take a walk. There's nothing more we can do for him; let the medical examiner take charge from here."

The Lieutenant raised slowly to his feet. The Captain rested his hand on Fisher's shoulder and led him out of the building and through the crowd of reporters and bystanders to the car. The two sat in the vehicle without saying a word to each other for what seemed like an eternity. Then the Captain broke the silence.

"Fisher, I need you, we owe it to Sergeant Fuller and the two other officers who died. I need my best man on this case to bring it to an end. Can I count on you?"

"Captain, I've never let you down before."

"I know you haven't, and I wouldn't want you to start now. Fisher, this thing has hit the ceiling. The

Commissioner and the Mayor are en route as we speak. They'll have many questions and we better have the answers. We have bodies all over this city and the Bronx and they're all tied together. There's also a shooting that occurred in Harlem earlier today which we can now positively tie to McCoy's gun. Two people died in that shooting and a third victim is in intensive care. Our suspects have been very busy. We've gotten one of them but there are at least two other killers out there still running free on our streets."

"Captain, I'll be fine; I'll see this case through to the end."

"Good, that's exactly what I want to hear. Now let's wrap up this crime scene and have something for the Commissioner and the Mayor when they arrive."

When Stepper returned to the hotel room, Carol was in the bed watching television. Stepper opened two bottles of beer, handed her one and kept the other for himself. They sat on the bed and drank together, not saying much, both lost in their own thoughts.

Carol looked him directly in his eyes and asked, "Stepper, wah you a go do 'bout de police dem?"

"Cho, from me born police a gi' me trouble, if I fi worry 'bout dem me would a lose me damn mind," he replied.

"Me just no want nothing happen to you. Me a think, we can go down south and stay wid me sister, me no haffi come back a Brooklyn, me wi' lef' everything right now if you want and go way wid you."

Stepper was touched by the offer, and for the first time he knew she had strong feelings for him. His main intent when he returned to the hotel room was to kill her and then head out to the Bronx, but she had touched a softer side of him. If he left her alive there's nothing she could do to implicate Chuckie or him in any of the murders, so why kill her? He dismissed the idea and realized that she would never know how close she came to being a homicide victim that night. He turned to her and held her hand. "Carol, me really appreciate that, but me have too much money tied up inna New York right now fi just lef' so, and besides, me no do nothing fi a run from de babylon dem. Wid a good lawyer me wi' clear everything up." He was saying whatever he could think of just to put her worries to rest. In more ways than one he knew he was a dead man.

Carol tried even harder to convince him. "Wah good is money when a man deh a prison or dead? You can make money anywhere you go. Just drop everything and mek we leave fi even a few weeks then we can come back and you take care of you business."

She was right and Stepper knew it. This was one of those crossroads and it could very well be the most important one of his entire life; it could mean the difference between his living and dying. He thought about his statement to Chuckie earlier in the day, *I nah tek no check from no police.* Chuckie did not hesitate to leave the safety of his home, knowing that he may not ever return to it, and he took that chance just to be by his friend's side. There was no way that Stepper could abandon his friend to run away to safety. The decision not to desert him was an easy one to make; he would rather chose death than abandon his friend. "Carol, as much as me would a like fi do that, me can't leave right now. I have fi take care a I business then maybe we can talk 'bout that."

Carol was disappointed. Nothing would please her more than to know Stepper was safe from the hands of the law.

Two of Stepper's closest friends were dead, he had to make sure that Chuckie wouldn't be the third. "Listen Carol, you alright wid me, you is a good woman. I no wan' mash up you life and bring you misery. Everywhere me go, trouble always follow me, you better off not thinking about I inna dem way deh right now," said Stepper.

"Wah you a talk 'bout, you a me man. You a de only man me a see and me no want lose you."

Stepper held her in his arms and kissed her deeply. He unbuttoned her blouse and removed her bra. She removed the rest of her clothes as Stepper got undressed, and then he held her naked body tightly next to his as they made passionate love as if there was no tomorrow.

Carol was asleep when Stepper emerged from the bathroom after taking a shower. He moved around the room very quietly, not wanting to wake her. After he got dressed he counted out a thousand dollars and left it on the night stand next to the bed. Then quietly he left the room. He checked his watch, it was 3:00 a.m.

Lieutenant Fisher sat facing Captian McKenny as they went over everything their investigation had uncovered in the past few hours. They ran Dreaddy's finger prints and came up with his real name, David Anderson. They obtained a search warrant, searched his home, and took in his live in girlfriend, Marcia Wayne, for questioning. With nothing to hold her on, however, they released her, but only after she revealed that Dreaddy's close friends were Stepper and Chuckie, and that he had a friend in the Bronx by the name of Pops.

Marcia was bitter about the loss of her man and she blamed his death on Chuckie and Stepper. In the past few weeks she had been trying, without any success, to convince Dreaddy to change his life and part ways with those two. Dreaddy argued that they were his only friends and that there was no way he was going to end his friendship with them, even if that meant losing her. She felt nothing but disdain for both Chuckie and Stepper.

Pops, on the other hand, was someone she didn't know much about so she couldn't provide much information to the Detectives about him, she only knew he lived in the Bronx.

The Detectives left no stone unturned in their attempt to find the identity of Pops, but they came up short. Ultimately however, it didn't matter because they had a clear cut case against Chuckie and Stepper.

Later they learned that Carol was missing from her apartment. The officers stationed at her house had somehow let her slip by them and the Captain was furious. He placed the responsible detectives on immediate leave, then put out an all-points bulletin for the arrest of Carol Wilson.

"Okay Fisher," said the Captain. "I want you to call it a night, get some rest and report back here first thing in the morning. It's 3:30 and there's nothing more we can do right now. I need you up and alert in the morning."

"Okay Captain, but I want to be placed on call if anything breaks while I'm at home."

"I will make that clear to the shift commander," said the Captain as both men made their way out of the precinct.

Chuckie stretched out on the couch in Pops' marijuana house. Baller sat in a chair facing him. They had seen the report of the shootout in Bushwick, it was big news. Both men were in disbelief that Dreaddy was dead. The news team now had his full name, David Anderson, a.k.a. "Dreaddy". Chuckie was getting worried about Stepper. He should have arrived by now but there was no sign of him.

Immediately after leaving the car wash, Chuckie had placed a call to his girlfriend, Dawn. He told her that Dreaddy was dead and that he would be away from the house for a few days, but that he would be in touch with her. She was very worried and wanted to be with him, but he quickly ruled it out. He told her to take his forty-four magnum and go to her mother's house to stay for a few days.

Chuckie called Cow next, explaining to him what he knew about Dreaddy, and told him to lay low for a few days since the police were sure to turn the Jamaican communities in Brooklyn upside down in light of the police killings. Cow assured him that he understood. Chuckie told Cow that he wouldn't be hearing from him for a few days, but that he'd eventually contact him to let him know where he could pick up his car.

Chuckie's mind was at ease as far as Dawn and Cow's safety, but he couldn't help worrying about Stepper. His mind wandered back to Stepper's girl, Carol, and he wondered if Stepper had gotten rid of her as he had suggested to him. He smiled as he thought about the hold that Carol had on Stepper. For the life of him he couldn't understand why Stepper would risk his life going in and out of the 90s knowing full well that Sammy and his boys wouldn't think twice about putting a bullet in his head. And on top of that, he took a police boy's revolver, turned the neighborhood upside down, and still had the nerve to go back there to see that gyal. "She must have some good obeyah."

Baller looked over at him. "Wah you say Chuckie?"

Chuckie laughed, "No nothing, me just a think 'bout a little gyal weh Stepper can't seem fi let go, no care how me a tell him fi shake her."

"Well you know, pum-pum a de down fall fi nuff man from God create this world. Look pon Samson and Delilah, Adam and Eve, and countless other men weh mek woman destroy dem life."

"Wah, you sound like a man inna him sixties wid nuff wisdom a talk like dat," said Chuckie.

"I grandfather I used to hear a say dat. It tek me a little while fi understand wah him did a seh, but now me fully understand and know seh a de truth him did a talk."

"De old man did right, and if only more a we could understand we wouldn't fall victim to a gyal like dat."

That little conversation helped Chuckie more than Baller could have imagined, it reinforced that the decision he had made to kill Ann Marie had been the right one.

Chuckie was far away in his thoughts when suddenly there was a loud knock. He and Baller both reached for their guns and eased over to the door. Baller took the lead as Chuckie followed closely behind him. Baller looked through the peephole and smiled as he saw Stepper standing on the other side of the door. Baller turned to Chuckie. "Stepper."

Chuckie breathed a sigh of relief as he reached for the door. His main man was finally there.

Stepper entered the apartment, it was 4:15 in the morning. "Yo, wah you a seh star?" asked Baller.

"Brooklyn a run red hot right now my youth, de police boy dem deh all over de city a pull over everybody weh look like a Jamaican just fi harass dem," replied Stepper.

"We haffi stay low fi a while till things blow over," said Chuckie.

"Right now I wrinkle 'bout wah happen to Dreaddy, I vex I neva deh deh wid him when de boy dem draw down pon him, me a tell de I dem, a nuff more police boy would a dead if I did deh deh," said Stepper.

"Me know wah you a seh, but we can't fight de entire New York police force, we haffi lef' New York fi awhile."

"Me understand wah de I a seh still, but before I do anything, I haffi get de boy Sammy," said Stepper.

"Wah Sammy have fi do wid I and I right now?"

"A him and him friend dem put de boy dem pon I and I."

"No tell me seh a de gyal Carol tell you dat."

"Listen man, dah gyal deh check fi I and I."

"Ann Marie check fi I and I too, but I mek sure she will never flip pon I and I. A bet you never get rid a de gyal Carol."

Stepper was caught off guard, he didn't believe Chuckie would have killed Ann Marie; he didn't know what to say.

Baller just sat there, not fully understanding what Chuckie was talking about.

Stepper felt bad. He knew Chuckie cared about Ann Marie, yet to protect the crew he had taken her life. It couldn't have been easy for Chuckie to kill her. He remembered the look of relief on Chuckie's face after rescuing Ann Marie from the hands of Mackie. Saving her life had been paramount in Chuckie's mind, and only a few short hours later he turned around and ended her life.

Stepper had the utmost respect for his friend. He kept quiet for quite some time not wanting to hurt his friend's feelings by saying the wrong thing, given the way he knew Chuckie felt about her. As far as Stepper was concerned however, Chuckie did the right thing. She couldn't be spared. They couldn't afford to leave her alive, and besides, Ann Marie knew exactly what she was getting into; those were the rules of the game they all played.

Stepper thought it was time to try and put things in their proper perspective. "Listen Chuckie, Carol no have nothing pon I and I, so I no see no reason fi get rid of her. Ann Marie on de other hand, was an eyewitness to four murders; we had no choice. Plus, everything change the minute Dreaddy kill de three police boy. You know how dem beast boy dem operate when one a dem get lick down, so you can imagine the kind a hell dem a go kick up wid three a dem dead, dem boy deh nah go leave no stone unturned. Carol couldn't tell de police boy dem nothing 'bout we, she no know nothing 'bout we."

Chuckie knew his friend was right, but he still would have felt more at ease if Carol were dead. "You right, this is a totally different ball game now and none a we no know how it a go end up. Right now we have fi stick together and make some wise move."

Stepper stretched out his right fist and Chuckie responded in kind. They tapped their knuckles together once, sealing their bond.

"Chuckie, right now we have a serious problem wid de boy Sammy. De boy a gi' police information pon I and I. De boy tell de police dem I name and send dem go a Carol house a look fi I. Me know de joker must a call you name too, me wouldn't surprise if a him why de police dem pull down pon Dreaddy. We have to take care a him once and for all."

"Alright, me know wah you a say, but we can't tek dem chance deh right now, things too hot a Brooklyn right now, and we have fi believe seh de police dem done have picture a we all over de place. Right now we haffi lef' de whole state a New York fi a while, me want we go chill out wid me cousin Devon a Jersey fi a while. Me want we catch the early morning traffic over de bridge, de police boy dem nah too check de traffic that time a de morning, because most a de people dem a go a work. Then we can deal wid Sammy and him friend dem another time."

Chuckie was right. They had to leave the city as soon as possible, lay low for a while and not take any unnecessary chances. Stepper knew it was the right decision, and not knowing exactly what the police knew about them made it even more important. It was just a matter of time before the police would tie them to Dreaddy; they already had the Volvo and by now they would have traced it to Chuckie. "The I right, a five o'clock now, we can flash in about a hour."

"Baller," said Chuckie, "Me ago lef' me brethren Cow Maxima wid you, me ago gi' you him phone number, me want you call him later inna de day and tell him fi come get it or you can carry it go gi' him a Brooklyn. Just tell him say I and I did haffi flash go out of town."

"Me wi' tek care a it."

An hour later the three men left the apartment together. Chuckie showed Baller where he parked Cow's car and handed him the keys. Chuckie and Stepper got in Stepper's BMW and took off for New Jersey.

Lieutenant Fisher's home phone rang. He checked the clock next to his bed, it read 5:15 a.m. He picked up the receiver. "Yea!"

"Fisher, this is the Captain."

"Yes Captain."

"I was just heading out the door when I got a call from our boys in Manhattan, they've got another body, It's that girl that rented the apartment on Eastern Parkway, Chuckie's girlfriend, Ann Marie Johnson. We've also come up with the name of a Jamaican guy in the Bronx who goes by the name of Pops. His name is Anthony Wright and he was gunned down on Sunday night. We believe the shootings in the Bronx were retaliation for that homicide. I'm just about to leave for the precinct."

"Captain, this could be the break we've been looking for. I'll be there within the hour." Lieutenant Fisher rushed out of bed, got a quick shower and was out of the apartment within minutes. As he drove he focused on how badly he wanted to get those guys, Chuckie and Stepper. It was now extremely personal and he had to get his hands on them. The more he thought about them the angrier he got. "To hell with going by the book," he mumbled under his breath.

Captian McKenny entered his office and was soon joined by Detectives Majors and Buchanan. The men knew they had to move fast to bring this case to an end. Time was of the essence if they were going to get their two prime suspects before they fled the state and possibly returned to Jamaica.

"Captain!" said Detective Buchanan, "I'd like to head out to the Bronx right away and aid with the investigation in the homicide of Ann Marie Johnson. I'd also like to question the girlfriend of this Pops guy. It's possible that our suspects may be hiding out in the Bronx given the fact that Chuckie's girlfriend turned up dead there. In fact, it's possible that he killed her himself."

"That was exactly my thinking, but for the life of me I can't understand why he would kill her," said Captian McKenny.

"Maybe he realized that things were getting out of hand and he wanted to tie up loose ends," said Detective Majors.

"That may make sense to him, but nothing a murderer does ever makes sense to me. I want Lieutenant Fisher to accompany the both of you to the Bronx. He's en route as we speak and should be here shortly."

"Captain," said Detective Majors, "I don't think we have a minute to spare; our suspect must be running scared by now, the murder of that girl proves it."

"I understand your concern, but I need a senior officer out there with you. This case has gotten a lot of high level attention in our state. We're under a damn microscope and we have to do this right."

At 5:45 a.m. Lieutenant Fisher entered the Captain's office. The Captain gave him a quick rundown on what was taking place, then ordered him and the two detectives, Majors and Buchanan, to head out to the Bronx immediately. By 6:00 a.m. they were in an unmarked vehicle. Detective Majors was behind the wheel with the Lieutenant sitting next to him. Fisher placed the emergency light on the roof of the vehicle, then hit the light switch. "Majors, I want to be in the Bronx in half an hour."

Detective Majors hit the gas, burning rubber as his vehicle leapt forward and out of the Precinct parking lot.

Chapter 11

By 6:00 a.m. Tuesday Chuckie and Stepper were midway across the George Washington Bridge and breathing a little easier as they entered the state of New Jersey. They weren't out of the woods yet, but they were a step closer now that they were out of New York. Not having to constantly look over their shoulders for the police, they could now turn their full attention to how to get out of the sticky situation they had gotten themselves into.

The sudden loss of Dreaddy weighed heavily on their minds. It was a major setback. Losing Pops was bad enough, but losing Dreaddy as well was devastating. Dreaddy had been with them for a long time before Pops joined their crew, and the bond they shared with him was unbreakable. Someone was going to pay dearly for Dreaddy's death, and Sammy came to mind as the perfect scapegoat.

Before leaving the Bronx, Stepper had offered Baller the chance to come and chill out with them in New Jersey, but he turned them down. He wanted to be there for Pops' baby's mother in case she needed anything. He also wanted to maintain the Marijuana house in order to keep a steady flow of cash in case anything jumped off that would require immediate funds. Chuckie and Stepper understood but warned him to be extra careful, as the city was now extremely hot for anyone of Jamaican origin, especially anyone tied to them. Additionally, Jolly's boys knew where the Marijuana house was and were sure to target it to avenge their comrades. Baller acknowledged their concerns, but felt that they wouldn't try anything with him. He assured Chuckie and Stepper not to worry; he was confident that things would blow over and not affect him in any way.

Stepper sat behind the wheel of his BMW, mindful not to exceed the speed limit. Chuckie sat next to him in the passenger seat with the Mac-ten laying on the floor in front of him, fully loaded and covered with a beach towel. They were each armed with a nine millimeter and Stepper was still in possession of the stolen police revolver. They rode in silence, each caught up in his own thoughts. They exited the bridge, then caught Route four heading west toward Paterson.

Chuckie broke the silence. "Yo, I man haffi check fi de youth deh Baller, eno."

"Yea, a good youth dat," replied Stepper.

"When I and I settle in we haffi send fi him."

"Yea, me no think it too safe fi him deh a New York right now and inna de weed house, you know de weed house a de first place Jolly boy dem ago want seek out dem vengeance pon."

"A dat me a think 'bout, it would a really hurt I if anything happen to him," said Chuckie.

"Yea, me feel de same way, but right now we haffi

stay low and out a sight fi a while, by now de beast boy dem must link we to Dreaddy and have out all kind a warrant fi we by now."

"You right, we can't afford fi stay a New Jersey fi too long, de boy dem bound fi link we yah so too. Me just want we chill out fi a few days and then flash go a Florida, and from deh so we can reach a Yard go chill out fi awhile."

"Yea, Jamaica a de best place fi we right now, we can chill out inna de hills and fire pon anything weh come up deh. Plus you know all a man need a Jamaica a some money fi buy off a few police boy and you cool."

"Yea," said Chuckie, "you right, we haffi mash a few works and load up pon as much cash as possible before we flash go a yard. De money weh we have now nah go last out deh."

"Me wan' we tek off de boy Sammy before we do anything. De boy fi good fi at least a half a million."

"Boy we just a run out a New York fi stay a step ahead a de police dem and you a talk 'bout go back deh already."

"You know, sometime de best place fi hide is right under a boy nose. Right now we no have too much choice, we have fi put we hand pon a big money before we reach a Florida."

"Alright, mek we reach a Paterson, and then see wah happen."

Lieutenant Fisher and the two detectives pulled up in front of the precinct in the Bronx.

"We have to meet with a Lieutenant Rogers of homicide," said Lieutenant Fisher.

The men entered the precinct and approached the

desk Sergeant showing their badges. They asked to see Lieutenant Rogers. The desk Sergeant made a call and then directed them to an office where they were greeted at the door by Lieutenant Rogers.

"Gentlemen, welcome to the Bronx. Come on in and have a seat."

The men entered the office and Lieutenant Rogers closed the door behind them.

"I'm Lieutenant Fisher from the 71st Precinct in Brooklyn, this is Detective Majors from our homicide division, and this is Detective Buchanan from the Special Crime Task Force in Manhattan."

"I've been expecting you. I've spoken to Captain McKenny from your precinct who expressed interest in a homicide which took place this morning. I was told it was tied to a quadruple homicide that took place in Brooklyn yesterday," said Lieutenant Rogers.

"That's right. We'd like everything you have on a Jamaican guy call Pops, correct name, Anthony Wright. We understand he was gunned down a few nights ago and we believe he is tied to the two suspects we're seeking in connection to those homicides in Brooklyn. Those two suspects, who go by the names Stepper and Chuckie, are directly tied to the assailant who attacked and killed three police officers yesterday," said Lieutenant Fisher.

"After speaking to your Captain I pulled his file and I have everything you need right here on my desk," said Rogers as he handed each man a file. "I have a team of detectives staked out in front of Anthony Wright's girlfriend house. She hasn't been seen at the apartment since the death of this Pops guy. We expect the family to recover the body sometime today from the coroner's office and we have an officer stationed there to bring her in when she shows up."

"I see here in this file that Anthony Wright was arrested for Marijuana possession on Gunn Hill Road six months ago," said Lieutenant Fisher.

"Yes, he was picked up on a minor drug charge, we believe he may have been selling it but we didn't have the evidence to charge him with sales. Subsequently the case was dropped. As you see, the address he gave us is the same address as his girlfriend," said Lieutenant Rogers.

"Yes, but as you know Lieutenant, most Jamaicans don't sell marijuana at their places of residence. I suspect he may have a place of business somewhere in that vicinity where he was picked up," said Lieutenant Fisher.

"I see he was shot on Gunn Hill Road, then rushed to the hospital where he died," said Detective Buchanan.

"Yes, that is my understanding. We don't have an exact address on Gunn Hill Road; we suspect it may have been a drive-by," said Lieutenant Rogers.

"Lieutenant Rogers, I would bet my entire salary that that guy has a marijuana outlet in that neighborhood; I'd like to take a look at the scene where he was shot. Also, I'd like for you to inquire with your narcotic detectives, if there is a marijuana house in that vicinity," said Lieutenant Fisher.

Any other time Rogers would have taken offense to officers from another jurisdiction trying to tell him how to do his job, but this wasn't just any case and some heavy hitters were involved. He was well aware that it went all the way up to the mayor's office. After all, three officers were killed in the line of duty. This could mean that promotion he had long awaited. His mood lightened with that thought. "Gentlemen," he said, "You have the full cooperation of this department. Everything is at your complete disposal. I'll work side by side with you while you are here in the Bronx, and, if need be, I will see this case through to a successful conclusion. We don't take kindly to cop killers here in the Bronx and I will do everything in my power to assist you."

"Thank you, Lieutenant Rogers. Your assistance is greatly appreciated," said Lieutenant Fisher.

Just after 6:45 a.m. Stepper pulled up in front of Chuckie's cousin's house on 12th Avenue in Paterson, New Jersey. The house made up a row of three family houses that stretched the length of the block. The neighborhood was a clean and quiet one, and at this time of the morning, with the kids out of school, there was no one out on the block except for a few people on their way to work. Chuckie handed the Mac-ten to Stepper before climbing from the vehicle. He walked up to the front door of the house as Stepper remained in the car, behind the wheel with the engine running.

Chuckie rang the bell twice to the first floor apartment. Within seconds he could hear footsteps approaching and then the door swung open. There stood his cousin, Devon, who was all smiles when he saw Chuckie. He knew that whenever Chuckie was around, there was money to be made.

From the car Stepper observed the scene, and then relaxed when he saw Devon standing at the front door. He cut off the engine, put the Mac-ten in a duffel bag and joined Chuckie.

The men entered the living room and finally started to relax. Devon idolized his cousin and would do anything for him; and Chuckie always made sure Devon was well taken care of. Many times in the past, after Chuckie had pulled off a job, he made sure Devon had enough money to pay his bills.

Stepper liked Devon a lot and would often visit and hangout with him for days at a time. Devon was a ladies' man, he had many girlfriends, and that appealed to Stepper as well. Devon often introduced him to many of the Jamaican girls in Paterson. Stepper took a strong liking to Paterson from the first day he visited the city; there was a large Jamaican community which made him feel right at home.

Devon loved Stepper's company; Stepper could do no wrong in his eyes. It wasn't long before most of the community became familiar with Stepper as he and Devon were often seen during the Summer months playing soccer with groups of Jamaicans in Eastside Park.

Paterson was one of the few places in America that Stepper felt he could let down his guard, though Chuckie was quick to remind him that he was slipping when he learned he was hanging in the park playing soccer.

Devon was well-known in Paterson. He had lived there most of his life and had graduated from Eastside high school. He had gotten to know Pops and Dreaddy through Chuckie and Stepper as well, admired them and considered them his close friends.

"Devon, wha' a gwaan?" asked Chuckie.

"No nothing, I should be de one asking unnu that."

"Right now we have fi stay low on yah wid you fi a few days, me no want you show no body say we deh yah."

"You know me better than that. A wha' a gwaan?" asked Devon.

"Dreaddy and Pops dead."

Shock and disbelief were written all over Devon's face, but before he could say anything Chuckie continued.

"Dreaddy lick down three police boy a Brooklyn last night. Right now me know seh dem a look fi Stepper and I, New York hot right now and we did have fi leave. You no see the news?"

"No, you know me no too watch no news."

"Well you better start watch de damn news and keep up with wah a gwaan round you, you never know when it may save you from go a prison," said Stepper.

"Man, me feel it fi Dreaddy and Pops, how it happen?"

"Some 'hurry come' bad boy lick down Pops a Bronx Sunday night, I and I draw down pon dem and done dem. Then we get caught up inna Brooklyn and haffi make some move, after de move Dreaddy tek I Volvo fi go lock it off and get inna a shootout wid de police boy dem. De police boy dem have me Volvo right now, so me know dem a look fi I hard," replied Chuckie.

"So wah unnu a go do 'bout de BMW, dem might know 'bout it by now."

Stepper and Chuckie hadn't given it much thought, but now that it was said it made perfect sense that the police could possibly have information on the BMW. They had to do something with the vehicle and not take any unnecessary chances with it.

Stepper's thoughts went to Carol. She knew he was driving the BMW. Would she betray him? He didn't think so, given the things she said to him in the hotel room. He wasn't too concerned about her, but he wasn't so sure about Sammy and his friends. They knew his car and were already giving other information to the police. Stepper had no doubt that they would give that information to the police as well, if they hadn't done so already.

"Chuckie," said Stepper, "we haffi get de BMW a new paint job right away, de nigga Sammy done know de ride. By now him must tell de police dem."

"Yea, that make sense, we can't tek no chance wid it," replied Chuckie. "Devon, me want you find a good place fi get de ride paint, and we need a place weh can do it fast. Me no want them have it fi no long time, we need it back right away."

"Yea man, me wi' tek care a dat today, me know a shop weh can do it, wah color unnu want it inna?"

"Wah you a seh Stepper?" asked Chuckie.

"Change it to a light color, green or gold."

"Alright, me wi' get pon top a dat right away," said Devon as he walked into the kitchen to prepare breakfast while Stepper and Chuckie stretched out on the couch and watched the morning news.

Lieutenant Rogers discovered from the narcotics officers in his department that a building close to where Pops was gunned down was, according to their informants, a location from which marijuana was being sold in the neighborhood. He obtained a search warrant and assembled a team of ten of his officers, along with the officers from Brooklyn, to serve the warrant.

It was 7:30 a.m. when the officers gathered in front of the apartment door. Baller was on the couch sound asleep when the door came flying off its hinges, but before he could reach for his gun he was looking down the barrels of several shotguns and automatic pistols.

"Freeze! Police! Don't move!"

Baller stopped short of reaching for his nine millimeter; he knew he didn't stand a chance. They had the drop on him and had him cold. He froze.

One of the officers immediately dragged him off the couch to the floor while another slapped a set of handcuffs on his wrists, and a third officer retrieved the gun from the couch that Baller was about to reach for. They searched his pockets and found a set of car keys along with five hundred dollars in cash. Once Baller was secured, the officers searched the apartment.

Lieutenant Rogers approached Baller. "Where are Chuckie and Stepper?"

"I don't know anybody by that name."

"Well it doesn't matter, we have you for four homicides committed yesterday, and if you don't cooperate with us, you will never see the streets again."

"I don't know what you are talking about, I haven't committed any homicide."

"If we say you did, you did; you know how we do it in the Bronx. Where is the vehicle that these keys go to?"

"They're my girlfriend's extra car keys, she has the car."

"Lieutenant, we've found about fifteen pounds of marijuana and another gun in the kitchen!"

Rogers and Fisher joined the officer in the kitchen.

"What've you got?" asked Lieutenant Fisher.

"It's a nine millimeter."

Lieutenant Rogers looked over the gun then looked over at Fisher. "Maybe we should run an immediate ballistics test on both of these guns."

"Yes, they may very well be connected to a few of our homicides."

"Take him in!" yelled Lieutenant Rogers to his sergeant, "And check all the cars in and around the building to see if these keys fit any of them."

"Will do, Lieutenant."

Baller sat in the interrogation room, worried. He wasn't sure whether or not the gun Chuckie gave him could be connected to a shooting. He was sure that it was not tied to the homicides committed in the Bronx, but he was worried just the same. It was now 9:00 a.m. and he still hadn't been given the lawyer he requested when they first got to the precinct. The cops had been drilling him nonstop for over an hour. They asked about Pops' killing, the Webster Street boys' murder, Dreaddy, Chuckie, Stepper and Barrington Davis, who they said owned the Maxima whose keys he had in his possession. He kept refusing to answer any questions without his lawyer present.

The detectives were getting impatient with Baller. They knew from their investigation and from the tenants in his building that he was in business with Pops. One of the tenants vaguely remembered seeing someone resembling Dreaddy entering the apartment sometime in the early evening on Monday. The tenant had further stated that there were two or three other men entering and leaving the apartment on Monday, but the tenant couldn't positively identify Chuckie or Stepper from the photos the officers showed him.

Lieutenant Fisher relayed everything back to Captian McKenny in Brooklyn who assured him that he'd have a warrant for the arrest of Barrington Davis within the hour and would bring him in for questioning.

Lieutenant Rogers hurried back to his office where

Lieutenant Fisher and the two officers who accompanied him were waiting.

"We got him! We have a positive match on one of the guns to the homicides in Bushwick."

"That is good news, we have the son-of-a-bitch. I have to relay that information to my Captain right away," said Lieutenant Fisher.

"Absolutely, we can now definitely place him with the other suspects."

Chapter 12

At 9:00 a.m. Devon slowly eased the gear of the BMW into first, then tightly gripped the wheel of the powerful vehicle, sensing what was next to come. He hit the gas pedal and propelled the car forward, burning rubber as he swung it out of its parking space. On his way to drop the vehicle off to be painted he felt good behind the wheel of this mean machine. Devon liked everything about the vehicle, including the black on black interior. He wasn't too fond of changing the color to green, he would have preferred blue, but it wasn't up to him. Someday he would own a BMW and it would be powder blue with white interior leather. He currently owned and operated a Ford Capri which he loved and took special care of, and it was a fine vehicle, but it couldn't compare to the BMW.

Since he had an hour before his appointment at the auto paint shop, he decided to visit one of his many girls to kill some time and show off the car a bit. He made a sharp right turn onto Main Street, just a bit too fast, and a policeman in a patrol car took notice and pulled in behind him. Devon saw him in the rearview mirror but didn't give him much thought. He kept driving, maintaining the speed limit, but then the officer in the squad car hit his lights. "Damn!" exclaimed Devon, as he pulled over.

The officer approached the vehicle with his right hand resting on the butt of his service revolver. "License, registration and insurance please."

Devon reached into his back pocket for his wallet, pulled out his license and handed it to the officer. Then he reached into the glove compartment to retrieve the registration and insurance and handed them to the officer as well. "What have I done wrong officer?" he asked, politely.

"You didn't yield at the stop sign back there."

"I didn't see the stop sign."

"Whose vehicle is this?"

"It belongs to a friend of mine."

The officer asked him to remain in the vehicle and then he walked back to his squad car. He returned a few minutes later and handed Devon his documents along with a traffic citation for failing to yield at a stop sign.

Being pulled over felt like a sign of bad luck, so Devon decided not to show off the car; he drove it directly to the auto shop without making any detours.

At the auto shop Devon picked out the shade of green he wanted, a mint green as Stepper had requested. He made a down payment for the paint job, then caught a cab back to his house. On his way home he thought about the citation he'd received and decided not to mention it to Chuckie and Stepper. He tore up the ticket and threw the pieces out the window of the taxi.

Captian McKenny assembled his team of officer in the precinct's briefing room. "Okay men, this is it. I have a search warrant for the premises of a Barrington Davis at 1721 Ocean Avenue, apartment D-5. He is not a suspect in any of the shootings at this time. His vehicle was found in the Bronx in the possession of a suspect who is tied to the Bushwick homicides. We have no current report stating that the vehicle was stolen, so we are to assume that he may have loaned the vehicle out. Don't take any chances. Our prime suspects, Errol Palmer, a.k.a. Chuckie, and Albert Roberts, a.k.a. Stepper, may very well be hiding out at that location. Approach the scene with extreme caution. I want every inch of that apartment searched and I want Mr. Barrington Davis brought in for questioning."

Cow sat at his kitchen table eating his breakfast and thinking about Dreaddy. *Damn, you're here today and gone tomorrow.* Cow had seen the news report on the shooting after Chuckie called him and he was steaming hot at the loss of his friend. If only he had suggested to Dreaddy not to leave his apartment that night, he may still be alive.

He was still lost in thought when the front door of his apartment came flying open, and within seconds he found himself surrounded by many armed officers aiming weapons directly at him. He was dragged to the floor and placed in handcuffs as officers spread out around his apartment. The officers also handcuffed Cow's girlfriend and sat her on the couch, and a female officer attended to Cow's son. The rest of the officers continued searching, leaving nothing unturned.

Captian McKenny entered the apartment once everything was secured. One of his officers told him that they had found a gun and some drugs - about 50 vials of crack cocaine. McKenny ordered them to read Cow and his girlfriend their Miranda rights and take them into custody.

Lieutenant Fisher and Lieutenant Rogers sat at a table in the coroner's office, and across the table facing them was Pop's girlfriend, Cherry Jones.

"Ms. Jones, I'm Lieutenant Rogers and this is Lieutenant Fisher. We are investigating the shooting death of your boyfriend, Anthony Wright. We need to know what you know about his shooting?"

"All I know is that he was shot on Gunn Hill Road, I don't have any idea who did it."

"Did your boyfriend have any enemies?" asked Lieutenant Rogers.

"Not that I know of, he was a very nice guy."

"Can you give us the names of some of his close friends?"

"He didn't keep friends, he was a loner."

"Well, we believe that the people who killed him knew him very well. I'd like to know if you've ever met or heard of a guy name Dreaddy?"

"No, I don't know him."

"How about a couple of guys by the names of Chuckie and Stepper?"

Cherry hesitated for a second, she knew Chuckie and Stepper did not kill Pops and she wondered what these officers were up to. "No, I've never heard of them before. Are they the people who killed my baby's father?"

Lieutenant Fisher felt Lieutenant Rogers was going about it the wrong way and was digging a ditch for himself, so he stepped in. "Ms. Jones, I'm going to level with you, there have been a rash of homicides in Brooklyn, Manhattan and the Bronx. Three police

officers have been killed by a close friend of your
boyfriend, a guy who goes by the name of Dreaddy, his
correct name is David Anderson. We believe he visited
the Bronx along with Chuckie and Stepper sometime
yesterday. They've killed five people in the Bronx in
retaliation for your boyfriend's murder. If you are
keeping anything from us, you'll be charged with
withholding information in a homicide investigation. Ms.
Jones, you have a child on the way, I would hate for you
to have to deliver that child in jail."

Cherry was getting nervous as she began to realize
how serious the situation was. Just in case the cops
already knew that Chuckie and Stepper visited her that
Monday evening, she decided to come clean. "Listen, I
don't know that guy Dreaddy, but yesterday Chuckie and
Stepper came to my house as I was coming from the
hospital."

Lieutenant Fisher's eyes widened, this was the break
he'd been looking for. "Ms. Jones, we need to know
everything that took place yesterday while they visited
you."

"They were not at my house for very long. They
asked how Pops was doing and I told them not well.
Chuckie gave me a beeper number to get in touch with
him and let him know how Pops was doing. I called the
number after Pops passed. He called me back and I told
him Pops had died, and that was the last time I heard
from him."

"Do you still have that number?"

"Yes, I still have it."

"Ms. Jones, we would like for you to come with us
down to the station," said Lieutenant Fisher.

"Am I under arrest?"

"No, we just need to check that number and have you call Chuckie from the station."

Cherry agreed to cooperate.

At 11:00 a.m., Chuckie, Stepper and Devon sat in the living room smoking a few spliffs with reggae music playing in the background, when Chuckie's beeper went off. He checked the code, it read 22. It was Cherry. He wondered what the hell could be up as he reached for a pen and wrote the number down. He turned to Stepper and told him that Cherry had just beeped him as he went into Devon's kitchen to use his phone.

Stepper stopped him just as he picked up the receiver.

"I no think it wise fi call nobody a New York from dah phone yah."

Chuckie thought about it for a moment, then replaced the receiver. "You right, but we haffi call her back fi mek sure everything cool wid her."

"Yea, we haffi call her back, but we haffi call her from a phone booth."

Chuckie turned to Devon and asked him to take him to a phone booth where he could return the call.

Devon drove for about two miles before pulling into a service station where he felt it was safe to place the call. He had the service attendant fill up his gas tank while Chuckie used the phone.

Chuckie dialed the number and the phone rang three times before Cherry answered on the other end.

"Cherry, how everything?" asked Chuckie.

Lieutenants Fisher and Rogers, and a team of officers listened in on the conversation. Lieutenant Fisher had coached Cherry on what to say to Chuckie to keep him on the line long enough for them to trace the call.

"Chuckie, Baller get lock up this morning," said Cherry.

"Wah, wah him get lock up fa?"

"Them lock him up fi a sell weed."

"How much a him bail?"

"Five thousand dollars, cash bail," replied Cherry.

"Alright, me haffi make a few calls and get de money together, me wi' call you back a this number in about a hour," said Chuckie as the operator came over the line asking for fifty cents more to continue the call.

"Chuckie don't hang up," said Cherry as the line went dead.

"Did you get a trace?" asked Lieutenant Fisher.

"He's calling from New Jersey, there wasn't enough time to pinpoint the exact location, but the call came from the Passaic area," replied the officer running the trace.

Lieutenant Fisher turned to Cherry. "You did good Ms. Jones, you're doing the right thing. We didn't have enough time to get an exact location on his whereabouts but we have it narrowed down. I would like for you to be here when he calls back."

Cherry nodded.

Lieutenant Fisher motioned to Lieutenant Rogers who followed him out of the office. "I have to place a call to my Captain. We need to get this information to the federal agents in New Jersey right away."

"I agree," said Rogers, "we have to keep them from leaving New Jersey undetected."

Captian McKenny picked up the phone in his office. "Captain McKenny here."

"Captain, this is Fisher."

"Yes, Lieutenant, what have you got?"

"We've made a major breakthrough in the case. We interviewed a Cherry Jones, who is the girlfriend of Pops. As it turns out, our suspects paid her a visit sometime Monday afternoon in the Bronx. Chuckie gave her a beeper number to contact him. We had her beep him from the precinct and he returned the call. We ran a trace but she couldn't keep him on the line long enough so we only got a partial location. We have it narrowed down to the Passaic area in New Jersey. We are expecting him to call back within the hour."

"Good work Lieutenant, I'll notify the FBI in New Jersey and have them get in touch with you in the Bronx to give you whatever assistance you need."

"Captain, did you locate the owner of the Maxima we found in the Bronx?"

"Yes. We have the owner in custody, a Mr. Barrington Davis. We recovered multiple drugs and a forty-five automatic from his apartment. We ran the gun and it came up negative for any of the shootings. Mr. Davis said he didn't know his car was missing. He last saw it on Sunday. Needless to say, I don't buy his story. We're still questioning him and we'll keep it up until he breaks."

"Captain, hold on to him, he may be tied to this somehow."

"I assure you, Lieutenant, I have no intention of letting him go. I know he's dirty."

"Captain, I'll be looking for a call from the feds. If anything else develops, I'll give you a call."

Chuckie and Devon returned to Devon's apartment

where Stepper waited for them. When they walked through the door the barrel of Stepper's nine millimeter greeted them, and they froze for a split second, just long enough for Stepper to lower his weapon.

Stepper could tell from the expression on Chuckie's face that something was wrong.

"Damn! Baller get bite."

"Wah dem bite him fa?" asked Stepper.

"De boy dem raid de base and bite him wid de weed. Cherry want we check her and put up de bail money."

"Man, we just lef him this morning to rawtid, how much a him bail?"

"She say de bail a five thousand dollars, me tell her me wi' call her in about a hour," replied Chuckie.

"We have fi do wah we can fi help dah youth deh, call Cow and tell him fi go check it out and pick up him car, you know him must a worry 'bout him ride," said Stepper.

"Good idea, before me call her back me wi' gi' him a call."

Chapter 13

Cow sat quietly in the 71st precinct interrogation room, a million thoughts running through his mind. He wondered if the gun Chuckie gave him was hot and why in the hell they just left his car in the Bronx like that. Did the police know that he was involved in the murders on Eastern Parkway? It was a good thing he didn't have to use the gun in that shooting. He wondered about his son and his girlfriend; his nerves were a wreck.

Detectives Williams and O'Connor entered the interrogation room. Captian McKenny stood on the opposite side of the one-way mirror allowing him to view the suspect without being seen.

Earlier they discovered that the gun found in Cow's apartment was clean and not connected to any of the homicides plaguing the city. All they would be able to charge Cow with was illegal possession of a firearm and possession of crack cocaine. Capt. McKenny was disappointed about how the case was unfolding with Cow. He'd been overly confident that the gun would be connected to at least one of the homicides. He pressed his detectives to pressure Cow to reveal what he knew about Stepper and Chuckie.

Det. Williams sat across the table facing Cow, while Det. O'Connor took a seat next to Cow.

"Mr. Davis, you are in a heap of shit," said Det. Williams. "We know Chuckie and Stepper were at your apartment as recently as yesterday and that you gave them your car."

Cow knew there was no way they could have known that. They were just fishing, so he kept his cool and responded carefully. "I don't know anyone by that name. I didn't even know my car was missing. I want to see a lawyer!"

"Listen, I'm tired of playing games with you," said Det. O'Connor who stood up over Cow and kicked away the chair from under him. Cow fell to the ground hard, still in handcuffs. O'Connor grabbed ahold of Cow's shirt and lifted him to his feet, then sucker punched him in his stomach.

Cow cried out in pain.

"You punk," said O'Connor, "I'm going to kick your black ass, but first I'm going to ask you one last time, what do you know about Chuckie and Stepper?"

"I told you, I don't know them. I want to see a lawyer!"

The Captain banged on the glass. He had seen enough and didn't want to run the risk of his department being accused of police brutality, especially when the eyes of the media were on this case.

The Detectives immediately responded to the banging on the glass. They acknowledged the captain by motioning to him, then exited the interrogation room. They met the Captain in the lobby, but before they could say a word he cut them off.

"Place him under arrest for possession of an illegal firearm and drug possession with intent to sell. Read him his rights and get him an attorney. I don't want this thing turning nasty with the news media looking down our throats. Is that clear?"

"Yes sir!" The detectives replied in unison.

Lieutenant Fisher and his team, along with some FBI agents, sat patiently along with Cherry as they awaited Chuckie's return call. "Fisher, he should have called back by now, you think he may have sensed something was wrong?" asked Lieutenant Rogers.

"No, I don't think so. We'll hear from him, I'm sure of it," replied Lieutenant Fisher as the phone rang. He looked over at Cherry. "Okay Ms. Jones, this is it, keep him on the line as long as possible."

Cherry picked up the receiver. "Hello!"

"Cherry, a me Chuckie."

"Yea Chuckie, me deh yah a wait pon you call, me think you never a call back."

"Sorry me tek so long fi call back, me did haffi take care a few things. You seh Baller bail a five thousand dollars?"

"Yea, him bail a five thousand dollars cash."

"Alright, me a go send a youth wid de money come check you this evening between six or seven o'clock."

"Me no know if me wi' deh deh that time, me haffi go over me mother house fi make some final arrangements fi bury Pops. Can him come any time sooner?"

"Me can't say fi sure, me a try get in touch wid a brethren a mine all morning and can't get him. Me figure by inna de evening me wi' hear from him and mek him gi' you a check."

"Alright, me wi' try me best fi deh deh a wait, but if me no deh deh him can just push de money under de door?"

"Yea, dat wi' work, me wi' show him fi do dat, and if you need any more money fi Pops mek me know," said Chuckie.

Cherry started to feel a deep sense of remorse at what she was doing as she realized for the first time just how much Chuckie loved and cared for Pops.

"Cherry.. Cherry! Everything alright?"

Chuckie's voice snapped her mind back to the moment, and she noticed that the officers in the room were staring at her intently. "Yea, everything alright, me just a think 'bout Pops," replied Cherry as she suddenly hung up the phone, hoping the officers didn't make the trace.

The officer running the trace held a thumb up and Lieutenant Fisher smiled.

"The call came from Paterson, New Jersey, 12th Avenue," said the officer.

"Good work," said Lieutenant Fisher as he turned his attention to the FBI agents in the office. The lead agent spoke up before Lieutenant Fisher could utter a word.

"I'm on top of it Lieutenant. I have my bureau chief on the line," said the agent.

Lieutenant Fisher turned to Lieutenant Rogers. "Rogers, relay that information to the Paterson Police Department, in New Jersey and let them know that I'm en route."

Rogers stared at him incredulously for a few seconds. Who the hell was he to start barking out orders in Rogers' department! Rogers almost told him to fuck off, but he caught himself as the thought of the potential for a promotion came to him. "Fisher, I'll make the call, but I'm damn well coming with you!" He didn't wait for a response as he turned on his heels and rushed to his office.

Lieutenant Fisher smiled. He knew exactly what was going through Rogers' mind. He would have felt the same way if the shoe was on the other foot, but this was a serious case; bodies were piling up all over the city! Someone had to take charge and bring it to an end. This wasn't the time or the place for formalities.

Lieutenant Fisher turned his attention to Cherry. "Ms. Jones you did a service to this state and I won't forget it. I'll have an officer take you home."

Cherry felt so bad; she hoped Chuckie would never find out that she had set him up. "Thank you Lieutenant, I have to make arrangements to bury my child's father."

After speaking to Cherry, Chuckie tried Cow's number again. This was his third attempt to contact him that morning. "Damn!" he uttered under his breath, "still no answer." Where the hell could he be, someone should have been at the apartment by now. He replaced the receiver in its slot and walked back to the car.

"How everything go?" asked Stepper.

"Me get her, me tell her say me a go send somebody come check her. But me can't get Cow, nobody no answer de phone."

"That no sound too right to me, you a try get him all morning and can't get him. You know Cow no too up and down pon de streets plus him no have no ride, and wid all wah a gwaan a Brooklyn right now him should a deh a him yard."

"Yea, me have a funny feeling something no right."

Stepper put the car in drive, pulled out of the space and headed back to Devon's apartment.

"Yo, mek we flash go a Brooklyn, me haffi find out wah a gwaan wid Cow, plus de police boy dem no know dah ride yah so we shouldn't have no problem," said Chuckie.

"Me concern 'bout Cow, but me no know if it wise fi mek dah move on deh inna broad daylight."

"Right now a de last thing de police boy dem would a look fi we a do, so that should mek it all the better fi wi' ease inna deh and see wah a gwaan. We can just hit the Garden State Parkway and mek we way inna Newark then catch the Holland Tunnel."

"Alright, but me wan' go pick up de Mac-ten a de house before we mek dah ride deh," replied Stepper.

"Yo, you know how me feel 'bout going backward, mek we just flash one time and done, you have you nine and me have me nine, plus you still have de beast boy thirty-eight right?" asked Chuckie.

"Yea, it inna de glove compartment. Alright, mek we flash." Stepper made a sharp right turn and headed in the direction of the Garden State Parkway.

It was half past noon as Chuckie and Stepper made their way south on the Garden State Parkway toward Newark, careful to keep within the speed limit. They hit Route 4 East to the Garden State Parkway South to Newark, then made their way to the Pulaski Skyway into the Holland Tunnel.

Lieutenants Fisher and Rogers and their team converged on the Paterson Police Department. They were greeted by Captain Paderewski. "Gentlemen, welcome to

Paterson, I'm Captain Paderewski."

"A pleasure to meet you, I'm Lieutenant Fisher from the 71st Precinct in Brooklyn, and this is Lieutenant Rogers from the Bronx." Fisher introduced the rest of his team to the Captain. The Captain shook each man's hand and then led them all to a conference room where a group of Paderewski's officers were already waiting. Maps of the layout of the city of Paterson covered one wall and stacks of paperwork, along with mug shots of every Jamaican that had ever been in trouble with the Paterson Police Department covered a large circular table. The Captain introduced the men to his officers and then got down to business.

"Lieutenant Fisher will you start by going over what these suspects are wanted for and why you believe they are in my city?"

"Thank you Captain. Gentlemen, we are looking for a pair of extremely dangerous Jamaican men. The two are wanted in at least eight homicides, and possibly in connection with two other homicides, all of which were carried out yesterday, Monday, in Brooklyn, Manhattan and the Bronx. A close associate of these two men was gunned down in Brooklyn yesterday after killing three police officers. These men are armed with Mac-tens and nine millimeters, and are known to wear bulletproof vests. One of the pair, "Stepper," a.k.a. Albert Roberts, along with a group of men, held up one of our police officers in Brooklyn Sunday morning, relieving the officer of his service revolver. Ballistics has positively matched that gun to several of the homicides. We've been pursuing the pair ever since. We set up a wiretap that we traced back to Paterson this morning. We believe these guys are laying low here in your city. The FBI has been working closely with us and we're committed to bringing this case to a close."

"Thank you Lieutenant," said the Captain. "We've gone to the location of the phone booth identified by you and have spoken to a few people there. We have a witness who positively identified Chuckie as being the guy he saw using the phone at least twice this morning. All my officers have photos and will be on the lookout for these guys. We are also checking with our informants in hopes that they may have something for us."

The phone rang in the room, the Captain picked it up and spoke to his officer on the other end of the line. After hanging up, he smiled as he addressed the men in the room. "Gentlemen, that was one of my detectives who informed me that Chuckie has a cousin living in Paterson, a Devon Maxwell. Mr. Maxwell was pulled over this morning driving a BMW with New York plates and he was given a ticket. I'll have a search warrant for his apartment within the hour. In the meantime I want surveillance on Mr. Maxwell's residence."

"Thank you Captain," said Lieutenant Fisher.

The Captain excused himself and left the room.

Chapter 14

Chuckie and Stepper parked their vehicle around the corner from Cow's apartment and made their way to the building on foot, walking on opposite sides of the street from one another and keeping a close watch for anything out of the norm.

Stepper made it to the building first and glanced around towards Chuckie who was just crossing the street. They entered the building together and climbed the flight of stairs to Cow's apartment. As Cow's door came into view they stopped in their tracks. A large police lock was on the door along with a "Do Not Enter" notice. They glanced at each other and slowly made their way out of the building without saying a word. There wasn't anything to say. They knew what had taken place and their main focus now was to get out of the building and the neighborhood. They retraced their footsteps back to the car.

Chuckie stopped short of the vehicle to cover Stepper as he got in, started the engine and unlocked the passenger door for Chuckie. They had done this routine on numerous occasions and had it down to a science; it had saved their lives in the past.

One day two of their archenemies had laid in wait for Chuckie at his vehicle. Chuckie had approached his vehicle without noticing the two men sitting a few cars down the street. When they saw Chuckie they rushed to react and didn't notice Stepper approaching Chuckie's vehicle from the opposite side of the street. As Chuckie approached his vehicle the two would-be assailants emerged from their vehicle with guns drawn. Stepper spotted them right away and opened fire, hitting them both. Chuckie also opened fire and both assailants died on the spot. From that day on, Chuckie and Stepper never deviated from that routine whenever they were together.

Stepper put the car into drive.

"Mek we flash go round a Dawn mother house and get Dawn fi mek some call and see wah dem lock up Cow fa," said Chuckie. "Her parents dem deh a work, so we will have de house fi tek care a wi' business."

"Yea, we can't just lef New York right now till we know wah a gwaan wid Cow, we haffi gi' Devon a call too, me know him must a wonder weh we deh."

"We haffi call him and mek him know we ago chill out over yah till it get dark before we head back a Jersey."

"Boy, it just come in like a one thing after another to rawtid, first Baller now Cow."

"Yea, you right, and we can't forget Dreaddy and Pops to rawtid," said Chuckie.

"Wah we ago do 'bout Cherry and Baller?"

"Good question, we might haffi send Devon wid de money go check her."

"When we tek care a everything wid Baller and Cow,

me want we get de Bimmer and hit I-95 south and lef this side a town fi a while, it just come in like we salt to rawtid," said Stepper.

"Yea, me feel de same way, when dem say dem ago done paint de ride?"

"Dem say we can pick it up Thursday morning."

The men then hit the Belt Parkway and made their way to Jamaica, Queens.

Stepper pulled into the driveway of Dawn's mother's house at 1:45 p.m. The neighborhood was quiet except for a few kids playing stickball in the street. Chuckie got out of the car and started up the sidewalk. Dawn was already at the door unlocking it as he approached. She leapt into his arms and gave him a passionate kiss.

"Woman, you act like you no see me in months."

"Me deh yah so worried 'bout you."

"Cho, you worry too much. Open de garage door so Stepper can park de car in deh."

After pulling the car into the garage, Stepper joined Chuckie and Dawn in the house. "Dawn, how everything?" he asked.

"A me should a ask you dat!"

"Chuckie wi' talk to you, right now me want use de phone." Dawn pointed toward the kitchen. Stepper found the phone and dialed Devon's number in New Jersey. Devon picked up the phone sounding nervous.

"Yo, wah a gwaan wid you," asked Stepper.

"Who this?" asked Devon.

"Stepper! Who you think, how you sound so?"

"Yo, me glad you call, don't come over de house, the boy dem a watch de house."

Stepper's heart began to race. "A wah you a talk

'bout?"

"Fi de past hour me see two beast boy dem a drive up and down de block. Me tek de tool and de weed and de money and ease out through the back a de house and lef everything wid me little brethren, Cat Man. You member me introduce him to you the last time you come check I?" asked Devon.

"Yea, de Yard youth weh live pon Graham Avenue?"

"Yea, a him me a talk 'bout."

"So mek you come back a de house?" asked Stepper.

"Me neva want unnu come back yah and me no deh yah, plus me no have no warrant pon me, so wah dem can do me. Listen Stepper, when me a come back a de house me walk pass de same undercover car wid two white boy inna it park down de street from de house, me gwaan like me no see dem and just walk pass dem and come inna de house, me just come in not even ten minutes now," said Devon.

"Devon, me want you leave de house and--"

Boom! Before Stepper could finish the sentence he heard a loud crash, then heard Devon shouting, "A wah de Bloodclot unnu a do yah!" Then Stepper heard the familiar command, "Police! Don't move!"

Devon slammed the phone down before he was tackled to the ground by two officers.

The line went dead as Stepper stood there with the receiver still against his ear. Tears burned his eyes along with pure hatred for all cops.

Chuckie and Dawn came into the kitchen and their sudden presence snapped Stepper out of his daze.

"Wah happen, how you look so?" asked Chuckie.

"De boy dem just run down pon Devon."

Chuckie couldn't believe it. "Wah! When dat

happen?"

"Dem just kick off de door as me a talk to him. Him show me seh him spot dem a watch de house over a hour ago, so him tek de business out a de house and lef wid one a him friend dem."

"Something no right, everywhere we go de boy dem tear down, somebody a gi' dem information."

"Yea, but how dem know say we deh a Paterson, no body no know dat," said Stepper.

"We tell Baller we did a go a Jersey."

"Yea, but we neva tell weh inna Jersey we a go."

"Yea, you right, plus me know say dah youth deh wouldn't gi' we up, dah youth deh a soldier," said Chuckie.

"It come in like de boy dem a hunt we hard, right now we inna a bad situation, most a de money we have we lef wid Devon."

"Rawtid, me neva even a think 'bout dat. How much money you have lef pon you?"

"Me have 'bout four hundred dollars pon me, and me have twenty-five thousand dollars lock off a I man gates," replied Stepper.

"Alright, me have de five thousand dollars fi bail out Baller plus Dawn have 'bout seventeen thousand lock off fi me. We can't go back a Paterson fi get de car. Right now we might haffi forget 'bout de Bimmer. Maybe later on Devon can pick it up. Me know de boy dem no have nothing pon Devon, if nothing, Dawn can check pon him and if anything she can bail him out."

"You right, but me no want fi just gi' up I ride so if I no have to," said Stepper.

"Yea, me understand wah you a seh. Right now we can't a drive round inna Devon car, de boy dem could a look fi it by now, we haffi leave it yah so fi now and get a rental," said Chuckie. He looked over at Dawn. "Dawn, me want you go rent a car, no get nothing fancy but mek sure is a good car, we haffi flash go a Florida fi a while."

Dawn didn't like what she was hearing, she was clearly worried, but she was a trooper. She had always been attracted to men that lived by the gun, so she was always prepared for the worst. For a split second, however, she wished Chuckie was one of those nine to five guys who never had a reason to flee from the police. She didn't allow the thought to linger, but went into the guest room where her things were and got dressed, ready to do as her man had requested.

Chuckie and Stepper had some serious thinking to do if they were to beat the law men hunting them. But first they had to gather up all the money they had and maybe pull off a robbery before leaving the city.

"Chuckie, me haffi reach a I apartment and get I money and some clothes. Plus before we hit de road me want draw down pon de boy Sammy, we can hold de boy and clean him out before we lef New York," said Stepper.

"Me did a think 'bout the same thing, de boy number finally come up, plus we owe him fi a work wid de police dem, but if things no look right inna de 90s, we haffi forget 'bout him and flash."

"Dat cool wid I man. Wah we ago do 'bout Cow and Baller?" asked Stepper.

"Good question, we can telegram de five thousand dollars to Cherry fi Baller. We can gi' Dawn de money fi send when she go rent de car, me ago gi' her Cherry number fi call her and mek she know say she a send de money. And she can check pon Cow and see wah dem have him fa."

"Alright, dat sound good, wah 'bout Devon?" asked
Stepper.

"We no haffi worry 'bout him right now, him mother
and de rest a de family wi' tek care a him, if dem no do it
me wi' mek Dawn bail him out. When we get a Florida
me wi' mek sure Dawn stay pon top a it and see if she can
pick up de BMW."

Dawn walked into the room and Chuckie filled her in
on the decisions he and Stepper had reached. He wrote
down Cherry's number and gave it to her along with the
five thousand dollars to be sent to her to bail out Baller.
Dawn called a cab service for a ride to the airport.

The Paterson Police Department SWAT team along
with agents from the FBI searched Devon's apartment
thoroughly but found no sign of Stepper and Chuckie or
anything connecting them to the apartment. They placed
Devon under arrest and read him his rights, and one of
the officers signaled Lieutenant Fisher and the rest of the
officers that everything was clear. Lieutenant Fisher and
his team entered the apartment and the head of the
SWAT team approached him. "Lieutenant there's no sign
of your suspects, and the apartment is clean. No drugs or
weapons."

"Thank you Sergeant, I'd like to speak to Mr.
Maxwell." He walked over to where two officers stood
guard over Devon. "Mr. Devon Maxwell, I am
Lieutenant Fisher of the 71st Precinct in Brooklyn.
Needless to say, you are in some deep shit. I'm looking
for your cousin, Chuckie, and his sidekick, Stepper. I
know they were here, so you better come clean with me
and make things easy on yourself."

"I haven't seen my cousin in months," said Devon.

"You were pulled over and ticketed this morning driving Stepper's BMW, so don't give me no bullshit. I will bury you deep under the prison if you fuck with me, boy!"

"I have nothing else to say to you. I want a lawyer," said Devon.

One of the FBI agents entered the room and handed the Lieutenant a receipt from Tommy's Auto Body Shop, dated that morning. He read it and smiled. "We got your ass. Now that we have the car we can give you a few of the murders that were committed yesterday in New York."

Devon started to sweat and his legs became weak and started shaking.

Lieutenant Fisher turned to the Sergeant and ordered him to take Devon down to the station.

Captain Paderewski obtained a search warrant for Stepper's BMW and sent a team of officers to the auto body shop to confiscate it. The vehicle was loaded onto a flatbed truck and taken to the New Jersey State Police Crime Lab where a team of officers went over it meticulously, retrieving fingerprints and anything else that might be evidence. They recovered four sets of prints, later identified as belonging to Chuckie, Stepper, Devon, and Stepper's girlfriend, Carol from Brooklyn.

Lieutenant Fisher knew that time was against him, and that every minute that passed enabled Stepper and Chuckie to put distance between themselves and him. He had to break Devon if there was any hope of bringing this case to a speedy end, but he was well aware that he had nothing concrete on him, and so did Devon.

As far as Devon was concerned, there was no way he would give up his cousin and his best friend.

Dawn pulled up to her parents house where Chuckie and Stepper were waiting for her. She had rented a blue Ford Tempo; it drove well and she was confident that it could make the journey to Florida. She hoped Chuckie would take her with him, but she wasn't holding her breath because she knew how protective he was of her; deep down she loved him all the more for that.

Chuckie was already at the door when she arrived. He had spotted her from the window the minute she turned into the driveway. He looked up and down the street for cops, making sure Dawn wasn't followed, but nothing looked out of the ordinary so he walked out to the vehicle as Stepper stood guard at the front door.

Dawn got out of the vehicle and greeted Chuckie, "How you like it?"

"It look alright, but how it run?"

"It run good, me no think you wi' have any trouble wid it."

Chuckie took the keys from her, got behind the wheel, started it up and took off down the street leaving Dawn standing in the driveway. He drove to the end of the block, made a u-turn and came back.

"It ride nice," He said, as he and Dawn walked back into the house.

Chapter 15

Lieutenant Fisher relayed everything that transpired in Paterson that morning to Captian McKenny. "I'm afraid we've come to a dead end with those guys. By now, I'm afraid, they could very well be anywhere in the damn country. But those punks will surface again Captain, and I assure you, when they do, we'll get them."

"What's the situation with the kid you picked up in Paterson?" asked Captian McKenny.

"We didn't have anything on him and he wasn't much help. I'm sure he knows something but he's holding out; eventually we will have to release him. I was assured by the Paterson Police Department and the FBI that they'll be keeping a close eye on him though. His phone will be tapped, and all we can do now is wait."

"The upside is that since we've turned up the heat the body count is down in the city. Let's keep it that way."

"The only good that came out of this is that those punks have gotten rid of a few bad guys for us."

"Really? Well why don't you give them a damn medal! Have you forgotten we've lost three good officers because of those thugs? Not to mention one of those officers being one of our very own - Sergeant Fuller!

And those thugs held up Officer McCoy and stole his service revolver which we still haven't recovered!" said McKenny.

"I didn't mean anything by it Captain, I'm just a bit tired and pissed off at not bringing this case to a close."

"Forget it. Why don't you go home and get some rest, there's nothing more you can do right now. It's up to the FBI to track those punks down now."

"I'll do that Captain, but I want to be on call if anything develops."

"I'll take care of that; you'll be the first to know if we get anything."

It was 8:00 p.m. when Chuckie and Stepper entered Stepper's apartment on Fulton Street in Brooklyn. Stepper retrieved the money he had stashed and gathered some clothes that he folded and placed into a duffel bag. He also retrieved a forty-five automatic and two boxes of cartridges.

"Yo, we can't stay yah so too long, we no know if de boy dem a watch yah so," said Chuckie.

"Nobody no know say I stay yah so, anyway me ready fi flash."

They left the apartment and returned to the rental car. With Chuckie behind the wheel, they drove to Eastern Parkway, then to Rochester Park, heading for the 90s. As they turned the corner to Sammy's building they saw Jah Mikes standing out front. They both noticed him at the same time, but unfortunately for Jah Mikes, he didn't see Chuckie and Stepper. The block was quiet except for a few people going to and from their homes.

"Yo, a de boy Mikes dat," said Stepper.

"Yea, a de boy," replied Chuckie as he drove past Jah

Mikes.

Jah Mikes wasn't familiar with the vehicle and paid no attention to it.

Chuckie and Stepper parked around the block from Sammy's building. They eased up on Jah Mikes with their guns drawn. Jah Mikes was caught totally off guard and there was nothing he could do.

"Wah happen Stepper?" said Jah Mikes, trying to play it off as if nothing was amiss.

"Don't move pussy!" Stepper frisked Jah Mikes, removed a nine millimeter from his waistband, and pushed Jah Mikes through the front doors into the building.

"Listen," said Stepper, "A no you we want a you boss, just knock pon de door and mek him let we in and we no do you notten."

Jah Mikes knew he had no choice and he wasn't willing to die for Sammy, but he wondered if they would really leave him alive if they decide to kill Sammy. Fear overtook him at that point and he decided to look out for himself.

"Listen Stepper, de boy Sammy a informer and me no want have notten fi do wid de boy, I a line him up fi rob him and lef New York."

"All right, we wi' rob him and gi' you a cut a de money, me know you know weh de boy hide de money," said Chuckie.

"Yea mon, me know weh everything deh." Jah Mikes made up his mind then and there that he was going all the way with Stepper and Chuckie. Jah Mikes knew Sammy had turned these men over to the police and that was a big no-no in his book. Plus, he'd always felt Sammy was short changing him and not paying him enough for his services. This may be his opportunity to get a chunk of money out of Sammy and cut ties with him once and for all.

The three climbed the stairs to the second floor. The lights in the hallway were dim but the building was clean, quiet, and well kept for the most part. Sammy lived in Long Island with his wife and children, but he kept this apartment as a stash house which he occupied with his girlfriend, Sonia. Jah Mikes was one of the few men allowed to visit the apartment; it was strictly for dropping off money and picking up drugs to supply the rest of Sammy's weed houses throughout Brooklyn.

Stepper had found out about the apartment from his girlfriend Carol who was friendly with Sonia. Sonia introduced Carol to Sammy, however when Sammy found out that Carol was seeing Stepper he forbade Sonia from associating with her, but by then it was too late. Carol had already visited Sonia at the apartment a few times while Sammy was with his wife in Long Island. He had no idea that Carol knew where the apartment was because Sonia had lied to him telling him that Carol didn't know where she lived. Sammy would have beat her senseless if she had told him the truth, and he may have kicked her out of the apartment and moved; she didn't want to take that chance. She made it clear to Carol not to visit her at the apartment again and not to tell anyone where she lived, and Carol agreed. But Carol hadn't mentioned to Sonia that Stepper had dropped her off at the apartment building a few times before, and that she had told Stepper the apartment's number.

Jah Mikes stood in front of the door, his heart was racing, and a thousand thoughts ran through his mind.

Stepper stood to his right, and Chuckie to his left. The thought of turning away from the door and running away from Chuckie and Stepper overwhelmed him but he quickly ruled it out. If he did run these men would gun him down without hesitation.

Stepper nudged him in the side with his gun and he rang the bell. Sammy came to the door with his gun drawn, as usual, and looked through the peephole. When he saw Jah Mikes he placed the gun in his waistband and unlocked the door. As Sammy swung the door open Stepper rushed him and knocked him in his forehead with the butt of his gun, knocking Sammy to the ground. Blood ran down his face as he let out a yell. Chuckie pushed Jah Mikes into the apartment, and Stepper was already removing the gun from Sammy's waistband.

Chuckie closed the door behind him and made his way further into the apartment. Sammy's scream sent Sonia running to the bedroom to retrieve the spare gun Sammy kept there. As she turned around with the gun, Chuckie stood at the bedroom door taking careful aim at her.

"Drop de bloodclot gun gyal!"

Sonia dropped it immediately. She knew she'd be dead if she failed to comply. Chuckie retrieved the gun from the floor, then marched her out into the living room.

"Stepper, how come you a do this to me?" asked Sammy.

"Shut up boy!" said Stepper as he ripped out a lamp cord to tie him up.

Sammy was in total fear for his life; he knew the reputation of these men and that he was as good as dead if he didn't play his cards right. His wife and kids were foremost in his mind so he decided, for their sake, to cooperate to the fullest. Better to live to fight another day, he told himself.

Sonia sat next to Jah Mikes on the couch, fear written on her face. Jah Mikes had always had a crush on her and didn't want to see her get hurt. Deep down he hoped Stepper and Chuckie would kill Sammy so at last he'd have a chance to have her as his own. There was no doubt in his mind that he could pull her if Sammy was out of the way. He'd always felt she was too good for Sammy anyway. He turned to her. "Sonia, no worry, everything a go alright, just do wah dem tell you fi do."

Sonia felt a little better hearing those words, she knew Stepper and Chuckie were known killers.

"Mikes weh de money deh?" asked Stepper.

"It inna de apartment upstairs, him have de key pon him."

Sonia glared at Jah Mikes, her eyes filled with hatred. Now she knew Jah Mikes had set Sammy up and was a part of the robbery.

"Jah Mikes, how you fi do this to me, me and you go way back," pleaded Sammy.

"You a informant boy, and no care how hard I work fi you you wouldn't even set me up wid a spot fi meself," replied Jah Mikes.

"You is a ungrateful nigga!"

Chuckie rushed over to Sammy and kicked him in his face. "Shut up boy, you set police pon I and I, and I man brethren Dreaddy dead because a you boy!"

"As there is a God me neva do that, how me fi a work wid police when dem a try put me out a business fi so long?"

"Me no inna no talk wid you, weh de key fi de apartment?" demanded Stepper.

Jah Mikes went over to Sammy, dug into his pants pocket and came out with a bundle of keys. He went through the bundle and separated a brass key from the bunch. "A de key this."

"Alright, mek me and you tek a walk," said Stepper.

The two of them went to the apartment upstairs and Jah Mikes unlocked the door. The apartment was completely unfurnished except for a couch sitting in the living room. Jah Mikes led Stepper to the bedroom. The only furnishings in that room were a queen size bed and a large storage trunk sitting to the right of the bed. Jah Mikes inserted a key and opened the lock, and Stepper ordered him to step aside, not fully trusting him.

Stepper lifted the trunk lid and revealed an AR-Fifteen semi automatic rifle along with three fully loaded magazines laying on top of piles of money and marijuana. He quickly removed the rifle, then turned to Jah Mikes. "Come in like you did want beat me to dah rifle yah?"

"Cho, how you can say dat, I man down wid de I dem." In truth, Jah Mikes was hoping to get to the rifle before Stepper so he could turn it on him.

Stepper wasn't fooled. He ignored Jah Mikes' response and turned his attention back to the trunk. The trunk contained thousands of dollars stacked neatly in one corner, and over three hundred pounds of marijuana. A total of one hundred and fifty thousand dollars was in the trunk. Stepper smiled. "Alright, mek we carry de trunk go downstairs." He put the rifle back in the trunk and closed it, then both men lifted it up and carried it to the apartment downstairs.

Jah Mikes knocked on the door and Chuckie opened it right away. "How everything go?"

"We hit de gold mine," replied Stepper, smiling. Stepper noticed that Chuckie had tied Sammy up even more; he was now on the floor, gagged and hogtied. Sonia was tied up as well, but not hogtied; she sat on the couch with her hands tied behind her back.

Jah Mikes didn't like seeing Sonia like that, he didn't want her hurt, but deep down he knew she could cause him a lot of trouble. He knew that she and Sammy had to die; that was the only way he could take over Sammy's drug operations without having to look over his shoulder.

"Jah Mikes, we a go mek you keep all a de weed, we a go keep de money. But right now you fi know say I and I have a major share inna de weed business wid you from now on," said Stepper.

The last thing Jah Mikes wanted was to have a partnership, and definitely not with these two killers, but he didn't have any choice. He was hardly in a position to object. "Yea mon, everything cool, me wi' handle de weed and mek sure the I dem get unnu money, de I dem can trust I pon dat."

Neither Stepper nor Chuckie trusted Jah Mikes but they were willing to give it a chance given that they didn't have anyone who they could trust right now to sell the marijuana. Baller and Cow were both in jail, and they were reluctant to leave such a large amount behind for the police to recover. Besides, Jah Mikes had held up his end of the bargain so far.

Stepper went to the kitchen and returned with a couple of large garbage bags. He placed the automatic rifle in one of them, then neatly stacked the money into the other.

Chuckie turned to Stepper. "So wah you ago do wid de boy and de gyal?"

192

Stepper didn't say a word. He pulled the police revolver from his waistband and walked over to pick up a cushion from the couch, then he walked over to Sammy, placed the cushion on top of his head, pressed the revolver against the cushion, and squeezed off one shot. Blood stained the carpet and Sammy went limp, dying instantly. Sonia screamed but the sound was muffled by the gag in her mouth. Stepper picked up the garbage bags and turned to leave.

Chuckie's voice stopped him. "So wah 'bout de gyal?"

"Jah Mikes in charge a her now, any problem wid her him haffi answer," replied Stepper.

Chuckie reached into his pocket and retrieved the nine millimeter he took from Jah Mikes. He removed the magazine, dropping it on the floor, then ejected the single round from the chamber and the bullet fell to the floor. He tossed the weapon to Jah Mikes. "I and I wi' stay in touch."

As soon as Chuckie and Stepper were out of the apartment, Jah Mikes reloaded his gun. He slowly walked over to where Sonia sat on the couch, tears filling his eyes. He quickly placed a pillow over her head and squeezed the trigger. Sonia's body went limp as she rolled off the couch to the floor. Jah Mikes cried as he placed all the marijuana into garbage bags except for a few pounds that he would leave at the crime scene. Then he retraced his steps and wiped down any fingerprints he may have left behind.

FBI Agent Peter Riley and two other agents sat quietly in their vehicle, observing the home of Dawn's parents, Mr. and Mrs. Albert, in Queens. In another squad car further down the block sat Detective Buchanan and Detective Bradley of the Special Crime Task Force. Both teams hoped this was the break they'd been waiting for. From wire taps they knew that Dawn was currently in the residence. The break had come when Dawn made calls to the Paterson Police Department inquiring about the arrest of Devon, and the retrieval of Stepper's BMW. The FBI quickly traced her call back to Queens, then placed a tap on her phone and set up surveillance of the residence. The wire tap revealed she was also making inquires about Baller in the Bronx and Cow in Brooklyn. The surveillance of the house had been in place for two hours.

At 10:00 p.m. Captian McKenny placed a call to Lieutenant Fisher, who picked up the phone on the second ring.

"Yea, Fisher!"

"Fisher, this is McKenny."

"Yes, Captain!"

"I have good news, we've located Chuckie's girlfriend. She's been making calls inquiring about a few of our guests. The FBI and our boys from Manhattan are surveilling her parents' home as we speak."

"Are our suspects at that location?"

"Currently it doesn't look that way, but we want to be on point if and when they show up."

"I'm on my way Captain," said Fisher as he hung up the phone and rushed out of bed and into the shower.

Chuckie sat behind the wheel of the vehicle as he waited for the light to turn green. "Stepper, we can't head south wid all dah money yah inna de car. If de boy dem stop we pon de road wid all a dah money yah dem ago tek it way and lock we up."

"So wah you suggest?"

"We haffi double back round a Dawn and lef most a it wid her, then she can fly down a bring it fi we."

"Cho, a you same one always a seh you no like go backward, and now you want we do dat. Me no feel too right 'bout dat."

"And you call me superstitious," countered Chuckie.

"I want tell you, me no know nobody weh can beat you in a dat department, all now you still a wear you voodoo chain," said Stepper.

"Me check seh you believe when you see me science a wuk yesterday inna Harlem."

Both men laughed as the light turned green and Chuckie made a right turn heading for Queens.

Chapter 16

The way Lieutenant Fisher barged through the doors of the Precinct, the officers in the lobby were under the impression that he was late for an appointment. He didn't make eye contact with any of them, but instead glanced quickly up at the clock on the Precinct's wall, 10:45 p.m. He hurried to Captian McKenny's office and knocked on the door before entering. Captian McKenny sat behind his desk and Detective Majors sat facing him.

"Good, Fisher, you've finally arrived. I want you and Majors to head out to Queens right away, I want you boys on the scene if anything jumps off. I don't want the FBI and the Manhattan squad getting all the credit if this case blows wide open."

"I'm ready to move out Captain," replied Lieutenant Fisher.

"Now I don't want you guys taking any chances. If our suspects show up call it in right away, is that clear?

"Yep."

Fisher and Majors retrieved a pair of shotguns from the property room before heading out to their squad car.

Dawn was in her bed in the guest room watching the

ten o'clock news and her parents were in their room a few paces down the hall. The thought of Chuckie weighed heavily on her mind but she felt some relief knowing that by this time he should be far away from New York and heading south. She figured she'd hear from him in a couple of days, if not sooner. She reached over, cut the television off, then said a solemn prayer for the man she loved.

Chuckie and Stepper turned onto Dawn's parents' block and nothing seemed out of the ordinary as they pulled up in front of the house. Chuckie got out of the vehicle with the motor still running, and Stepper sat in the passenger seat, the AR-Fifteen on the floor at his feet.

As Chuckie climbed the steps to the front door he felt a sudden sharp pain in his neck - the same pain he felt that night in Harlem. A sense of dread came over him. He held on to his gun and his thoughts turned to Dawn and whether she was all right. He quickly rang the bell.

As the car came down the block, Agent Riley's eyes were drawn to the vehicle. He couldn't make out the faces in the dark, but he quickly wrote the license plate number down as he'd done with every vehicle they had seen over the past two hours. He knew immediately that it was a rental vehicle and he started to relax when suddenly his heart skipped a beat. "Damn! That's them!"

The vehicle came to a full stop in front of Dawn's parents' house. The two men in the vehicle had to be Chuckie and Stepper. Agent Riley picked up his radio and called it in. Buchanan took the call.

"Buchanan, we have movement, it looks like our suspects."

"Yea, Riley, we're on top of it, but we can't make out the faces of the two occupants in the vehicle."

"Wait! I have a positive I.D. on the driver, he's the one called Chuckie; he's making his way to the front door," said Agent Riley.

"We need to call it in and request backup on this one."

"We have enough men to take them down right now, we can't wait for fucking backup! We cannot allow them to slip away," yelled Riley.

"I'm calling it in. Don't make a move until we get the go ahead," said Buchanan.

Agent Riley didn't respond. He replaced the radio then reached over to the glove compartment and retrieved a mobile phone which he used to punch in four digits. Those digits alerted his division that he was in need of backup. His location was already on file. He picked up the radio again. "Buchanan, I've made the call. Follow my lead. We are not waiting for the damn cavalry."

"Okay! You're calling the shots on this one."

"I'll take full responsibility for everything; follow me." Agent Riley put his car into drive and took off from the curb heading straight for Chuckie's vehicle with his high beams on. Detective Buchanan followed his lead coming from the opposite direction.

Stepper saw the two vehicles bearing down on him at high speed. He grabbed the rifle and released the safety latch.

Chuckie had just rung the bell when he heard the sound of the speeding cars approaching. He spun around to see the two vehicles racing towards him. He pulled out his nine millimeter and opened fire on the cars, emptying his magazine.

Stepper emerged from the vehicle, placed the AR-Fifteen on top of the car and squeezed off a steady burst. Both vehicles came to a screeching halt and the officers emerged in an attempt to find cover behind their vehicles. One of the FBI agents already lay dead in the vehicle from a gunshot wound to his forehead. Agent Riley and the remaining FBI agent returned fire.

Detective Buchanan screamed for assistance on his radio. "Officer down! Officer down!"

Dawn heard the doorbell and went to the window to see who it was. When she saw Chuckie, her heart and mind raced. Then out of the corner of her eye she saw the two cars speeding towards Chuckie. She knew right away who they were and an alarm went off in her mind. She saw the reaction on Chuckie's face as he reached for his gun and started to fire on the approaching vehicles. All she could think of doing at that moment was to call out, "Chuckie! Chuckie! Run!"

Chuckie couldn't hear her shouting over the sound of gunfire that filled the quiet neighborhood. He made his way back to the car where Stepper had positioned himself with the rifle.

"Yo, we haffi get out a yah, de boy dem ago swarm de area soon," said Stepper.

"Yea, me know, but if we try go back inna de car we ago inna de open, we haffi lef' yah pon foot."

"Alright, reach in and grab de duffel bag wid de money and de rest a tool dem, me wi' cover you." Stepper opened up a steady burst of fire on the officers and Chuckie stayed low enough to reach into the vehicle in an attempt to retrieve the duffel bag.

The officers seized the moment and opened up with everything they had. The car glass shattered all around Chuckie and Stepper, but somehow Chuckie was able to reach in and pull out the duffel bag without getting hit.

"Alright, me a go cover you, make you way down de block then you cover me," said Stepper.

Chuckie reached into the duffel bag and retrieved a fifteen shooter nine millimeter along with the one he already held, and he hoisted the duffel bag over his shoulder. With both nine millimeters at the ready he gave Stepper the go ahead.

Stepper eased over to the hood of the car and opened up on everything that moved.

Chuckie raced for a set of parked cars a few doors down the street. Agent Riley and the other officers stayed low as the AR-Fifteen rattled their cars, shattering the windows and leaving gaping holes in the their vehicles.

The first set of sirens sounded and Stepper and Chuckie knew that time was against them.

As he neared Queens, Lieutenant Fisher heard Detective Buchanan's call for assistance and floored his vehicle. He turned onto the block and was greeted by the sound of rapid gunfire. "Damn, those sons-of-bitches have automatic weapons!" Fisher put his vehicle in park, blocking off the street. He and Detective Majors managed to work their way to the officers who were pinned down as other squad cars also filed into the area.

Chuckie opened up with both nine millimeters blasting, which signaled Stepper to make his move. He dashed over and took cover next to Chuckie. The officers returned fire and fanned out to prevent Chuckie and Stepper from escaping. Chuckie raised up from behind the car and caught a glimpse of Detective Buchanan racing across the street. Chuckie let loose a barrage of shots in his direction, and two of them found their target hitting the detective in the leg and upper torso. His bulletproof vest saved his life as he fell flat in the middle of the street. Sirens sounded from every direction.

"Chuckie, we haffi move, we can't stay yah so!"

"Cover me," said Chuckie.

Stepper opened up with the rifle as Chuckie ran for a fence leading to a yard. Lieutenant Fisher and Detective Majors read the move and opened up at the same time with shotgun blasts, hitting Chuckie as he was about to scale the fence. Chuckie fell to the ground, blood pouring from both his legs. His vest had taken most of the pellets, but a few tore through his legs hitting the main artery in his left leg; he was bleeding badly. Stepper reloaded the rifle and sprayed anything that moved as he made his way over to Chuckie. "Chuckie, hold on to me, we can't stay up against de fence!"

Chuckie held on to Stepper with all his might, then the both of them attempted to make it away from the fence to the cover of a nearby car. As Stepper stood up with Chuckie holding onto him, a shot rang out from an FBI sharpshooter. The bullet grazed Stepper's neck and landed square into Chuckie's head. Stepper felt the force of the impact as it knocked Chuckie back up against the fence. Stepper knew his best friend was dead, but he had to make sure. Not concerning himself with the wound to his neck, or the fact that he was still in the open, he kneeled next to his friend. "Chuckie! Chuckie!" There was no response. The back of Chuckie's head was blown away clean and blood soaked the pavement; he was gone. Stepper glanced down at the ground. There laying next to

Chuckie was the chain, that damn voodoo chain. Somehow it came free from around Chuckie's neck, but the chain wasn't broken, he could see clearly that all the links were still intact.

He snapped quickly back to the situation at hand and his reflexes and drive to survive kicked in. He reached down and snatched the duffel bag away from Chuckie's lifeless body, then picked up the chain and shoved it into his pocket. He raced for the fence nearest to him, and just as he reached the fence and climbed onto it, a shot rang out. The force of the impact carried him completely over the fence where he fell flat on his face. A sudden unbearable pain rushed through his entire body. He summoned every fiber of his being for the strength and energy to get to his feet, but to no avail; it was over.

Stepper turned toward the duffel bag. It was split open and money flew everywhere. He smiled as everything around him went black.

The End

GLOSSARY

Jamaican Patois is a colorful and animated language not only spoken as a means of communication, but also as an expression of a very passionate, proud and unique people. This glossary is meant to clarify the usage of dialect used in this novel and is by no means a complete or comprehensive depiction of the language.

A: it is, of
Ago: to go, I am going, to do

Babylon: police officer
Beast boy: police officer
Bite: to get caught/arrested
Bloodclot: an insult used to show anger
Bredda: brother (term of endearment
Breed off: to get pregnant, impregnate
Brush: kill
Buddy: male private part, genitals

Chain: necklace
Check: to visit someone, think, believe
Check fi: to like someone
Cho: showing disappointment

Dah: that
Dat: that
De: the
Deh: there, to be somewhere
Deh deh: is there, over there
Dem: them
Draw card: to fool someone

Dutty: dirty

Eat: get money
Eno: you know

Fa: for
Fi: to, for
Fi get hold: to get caught
Flash: move quickly
Fly off: start up
Food: money
Fuckery: wrong, unfair

Gi': give
Gwaan: happening, going on, go on
Gyal: girl

Haffi: have to
Hay: hey
Him a sleep: to let down one's guard
Hurry come: amateur

I: my, me, I'm
I man: I
Inna: in, into

Jam: hang out

Lef: left, to leave
Lick: hit
Licky-licky: greedy

Mash: do, complete
Me/Mi: my, I, I'm, mine
Mek: make
Meself: me, myself
Mon: man

Nah: no, not
Neva: never
Nine: nine millimeter gun
Notten: nothing
Nuff: a lot, many
Nuh: no, not, don't

Obeyah: Caribbean slang for voodoo

Pitch: kill
Pon: on
Pum-pum: a woman's genitals
Puppa: a term of endearment

Raas: "really?", "damn!"
Rawtid: a common mild expletive of surprise or vexation, as in, wow, gosh or heck
Red hot: nonstop
Rope in: pull in close, bring closer

Salt: cursed, to have bad luck

Seh: say
Show: tell
Spliff: large cone-shaped marijuana cigarette

Teeth: bullets
Tek: take, took
Thing: a girl
Tool: gun

Unnu: you all, your

Vex: upset

Wan': want
We: us, we
Weed: marijuana
Weedhouse: a place where marijuana is sold
Weh: where, that, why
Wha/Wah: what
Wi': will
Wid: with
Works: job
Wrinkle: upset
Wuk: work

Yah: here
Yard: Jamaica
Yo: hey, hello
Youth: young man

ABOUT THE AUTHORS

T. Anthony Johnson and K.M. Johnson enjoy writing fiction with Jamaican themes. As Jamaican immigrants themselves, they are uniquely qualified to communicate the struggles endured by immigrants trying to make a life in America.

"Jamaican Steppers" is their first installment of Jamaican themed novels, depicting a variety of Jamaican characters and the action-packed lives some live. Buckle up as these exquisite story tellers take you on a roller coaster ride that will leave you breathless.

17189824R00129

Made in the USA
Middletown, DE
10 January 2015